About the author

Gillian Thornhill is a retired teacher of languages living in North Yorkshire. Her interests include reading, music especially opera, writing, film, travel, theatre, and interacting with friends in the English countryside.

THE DECISION

Gillian Thornhill

THE DECISION

Vanguard Press

A CIP catalogue record for this title is
available from the British Library.

ISBN 9781784656652

*Vanguard Press is an imprint of
Pegasus Elliot MacKenzie Publishers Ltd.*
www.pegasuspublishers.com

First Published in 2019

**Vanguard Press
Sheraton House Castle Park
Cambridge England**

Printed & Bound in Great Britain

Dedication

This book is dedicated to the descendants of Jacob and Maria, and those like them.

Chapter 1
Lodz 1923

Jacub Mendelson peered out of the dingy window overlooking Zierska Street, and noticed familiar smoke belching out of the city's factories on another overcast, gloomy February morning. The snow that had fallen thick yet again had been followed by a temporary thaw, filling the pavements and roads with ankle-deep, muddy slush, invading all but the sturdiest footwear. The temperature would probably drop again, resulting in black ice, dangerous for his mother on her shopping day or when she visited the sick at the Jewish Hospital.

It was eight thirty. He sighed, and after a brief breakfast of lemon tea and slices of rye bread, he ventured out onto the courtyard lying between the tenement buildings. His father, Ezra, had already long gone to help out with the fruit and vegetable delivery for his stall on the Baluty market square, and his wife, Miriam, employed at one of the many textile factories in the city, had also crept out earlier to start her shift. With shoulders hunched up against the cold, he made his way to the small shop he rented on Piotrowska Street. He felt disconsolate, pessimistic even, knowing only too well that he would sell very little merchandise on that day, or any other come to that, yet rent had to be paid and food to be bought.

Winter could be cruel in Poland, and the greyness of the tenement buildings depressing, he thought, as he crossed the courtyard to reach Zgierska Street. The war had knocked the stuffing out of Lodz. The German occupiers had stripped the factories of parts and raw materials, and now the city, devoid of investment to modernise, could not keep pace with the world-wide textile market. It just wouldn't happen. Russia had been their main trading partner, but World War I and the 1920 war had put paid to that. This last was over land borders and the creeping menace of Bolshevism. Poland had won, but at a cost to the trade. Prices of everything had gone up, so that there was less trade within the country itself.

Lodz, Poland's second city after Warsaw, with its textile industry, was known as the Manchester of Poland. After World War I, many Jews, whose families had lived in shtetls in the Pale of Settlement for generations, moved from the countryside to the city in search of work at the end of the Great War, and swelled the population of job seekers. The Jewish citizens numbered two hundred and thirty-three thousand, roughly one third of the entire population, resulting in too many applicants for too few jobs. Jews were doubly disadvantaged by the tax system and by the discriminatory policies of the State with regard to capital investment. Some managed to develop their factories with foreign investment, but pitifully few. And then again, trade was the occupation that most suffered from boycotts and antisemitic riots on market days and at fairs in Poland.

The Mendelson family were secular Jews, and not

members of a synagogue, but attended shul for Rosh Hashanah, Yom Kippur and Pesach. Apart from these major festivals, their last attendance had been for the wedding of Jacub and Miriam at the Great Synagogue on Spacerowa Street. It was a reformed congregation in one of the largest buildings in that smoke-filled city. That was three years ago, and Jacub smiled at the memory of Miriam, radiant in her white dress, looking up at him from under the chuppah with such dreamy love and devotion until the smashing of the glass and Mazel Tov brought her back to reality! They had been childhood sweethearts, looked at nobody else and remained steadfast to each other. No matchmaker or arranged marriage was needed for them. Somehow providence had smiled on them. Their union pleased both their parents, and it was agreed that Miriam would move into the Mendelsons' house, enabling Jacub and his bride to save for their own home in the not too distant future... but three years later their hopes and aspirations had not come to fruition, and they longed for privacy in their own place.

The Mendelson home was large compared with those across town where thousands of Hasidim lived in cramped poverty and hunger, with no running water or sewerage system. Yet Jacub and Miriam had a small room to themselves, as did Shimon, Jacub's younger brother; then apart from his parents' room, Grandmother shared hers with a loom used by the family to produce cloth for sale in Jacub's shop. A good idea in theory, but, despite the mixed population of Poles, Jews, Germans and Russians, little money was to be made, and whenever economic hardship raised its ugly head, then so did antisemitism. It was always there; it just got worse.

After a few hours of rearranging the knitted garments in his shop window in the hope of enticing potential customers within, followed by a general tidying up of his stock, Jacub locked up and went to help his father on the fruit and vegetable stall. He could be more help there, clearing away and stacking boxes before light faded. It was Friday afternoon, and all Jews, secular or Orthodox, observing the Sabbath ritual, hurried home before sundown, the Orthodox uniformly recognisable in their black suits and hats, or shtreimel, moving quickly in and out of the stalls with their produce, to head for home. Most were very poor; in fact, eighty per cent of the Lodz Jews were poor, yet their children were numerous.

If we let the shop go, and simply sell our knitwear on a stall, we can save money, Jacub thought to himself. He would talk it over with Miriam that evening, and he knew she would agree. Their original, ambitious idea of opening the shop had proved unsuccessful, so they had to accept the fact and move on. The quality of the merchandise was good, but at unaffordable prices except to the occasional visitor. Even then the profit margins were too narrow for comfort.

Jacub, together with Ezra, arrived home well before sundown, in time to see his mother place the silver candlesticks on the table, with two loaves of challah covered with a napkin next to a glass of wine on a spotless white tablecloth. Then when the whole family was ready... Ezra, Jacub, Shimon, Miriam and Grandmother... Sara lit the candles, waved her hands over them to welcome in the Sabbath, and covered her eyes before reciting the blessing.

"Barukh atah Adonai Elohaynu melech ha-olam. (Blessed are you, Lord our God, King of the Universe)."

Sara had cooked and prepared cholent for Shabbat, a dish of baked meat and vegetables, and now for twenty-four hours they would rest and abstain from work. The Mendelsons did not observe this rule too stringently, like some of their friends and neighbours. To some extent it was paying lip service and identifying as Jews which they were all proud to be, despite the hatred which sometimes confronted them.

At bedtime Jakub and Miriam whispered together in their modest room about letting the shop go, and how storing merchandise in the house would be difficult and they also realised that in selling the items on a stall, they would inevitably make a loss. At least they would save on the rent. They resolved not to tell their parents until they were sure of their own plans.

Miriam's lovely face was very pale, and blue shadows had puffed up around her eyes, spelling out lack of sleep and her woman's time but also sadness. Both families were expecting her to produce a baby; after all, it had been three years, but for whatever reason she did not get pregnant. Her woman's time just continued relentlessly on its heartbreaking, repetitive rhythm, and each month she could not hold back her tears. She cried in Jakub's arms, but not too loudly so as not to be heard by her in-laws.

Of course, she felt as if she was letting everyone down, but particularly Jacub who she knew so wanted a son; the pressure never left her, and she thought it might worsen rather than improve. Then it seemed that all her friends and acquaintances of around her age had married in the same year and had now given birth to their second or third child. Comments were made, and they hurt.

"Thy wife shall be as a fruitful vine." She knew the quotation from the Book of Psalms, and she also knew that procreation was one of the main purposes of marriage, and according to the Book of Leviticus, barrenness was a curse and a punishment. In the Book of Genesis, Rachel had preferred death to childlessness.

Miriam couldn't fathom why she had not conceived. She viewed children as a gift from God, and, in withholding a child from her, surely the Almighty was punishing her for something. But for what? She had always tried to be a good daughter, a loving wife and daughter-in-law, so what could be the reason for this punishment? Was it because she did not go to shul often enough?

Jacub was always sympathetic, but he, too, could not understand their lack of fertility, and became embarrassed by his parents' hints and optimistic expectations. For several reasons he wished they could avoid the pressure not only from his parents and Miriam's, but also from the Jewish community in their neighbourhood.

It seemed that the need to make an important decision had dawned on them both at the same time, and that decision was to leave Lodz and travel to Berlin to start a new life. There they hoped to be able to free themselves from relative poverty, from Polish antisemitism and the stress of not producing a baby; a chance to be themselves and rent their own place. They agreed to say nothing to Ezra and Sara or to Miriam's parents until their plans had become more organised and definite. The first task, after contacting the landlord to cancel the shop rental, was to obtain passports which would mean sending their papers to the Ministry of the Interior in Warsaw.

Each day they both tried to do something towards their new goal which filled them with the nervous excitement of anticipation. Miriam continued with her job at the factory, whilst Jacub hired a stall in the market to sell off the knitwear from the shop. Fortunately, with cut-down prices, the merchandise was much easier to sell.

Grandmother, Sara, Ezra and Shimon all sensed that Jacub and Miriam were making plans, but what was it? Had Miriam finally become pregnant, and was about to break the news to them perhaps on the next Shabbat?

Jacub's friend, David Blomberg, had recently returned to Lodz from Berlin after a short stay, and was full of praise and information regarding the situation there. Despite unemployment, hyperinflation and street riots, since the 14–18 war many Ostjuden (eastern Jews) had moved there from Poland, Lithuania and Russia to enter all segments of society. Life, he said, was more just under the Weimar Democratic Republic, the Germans were struggling to build up the country again after an ignominious defeat, and that it was possible for Jews to move across the border and stay indefinitely. Plenty of his friends from Lodz had already taken the decision to go; in fact, it might be possible to join a group on a hired vehicle and travel directly to Berlin, sharing the cost with the other passengers, and departing from near the Great Synagogue. The journey would take several hours, with stops on the way, and, of course, at the border, but there would be no difficulty in finding temporary accommodation in the Jewish Scheunenviertel area of Berlin, until they properly organised themselves and settled in their own place.

The plans were finally revealed to the family at the next Shabbat who were totally surprised and secretly disappointed that their news did not include a forthcoming birth. Grandmother was philosophical about their plans, understanding the needs of young people, and Shimon's world did not revolve around babies. He was the intellectual of the family and loved to read and study the Torah, in fact he seemed to be verging towards Hasidism, much to the consternation of his secular family. Ezra and Sara, however, were disappointed that they would not only lose their son and daughter-in-law to Berlin, but also any grandchildren to be born in the future. They also knew that distance and cost would prevent them from visiting often. Oy vey, if that is God's will, then they must accept it, but it was hard.

When Miriam broke the news to her own parents, Samuel and Esther Biderman, they were also disappointed about their departure to Berlin, but less so than the Mendelsons since Miriam came from a large family, and her five sisters had already produced several grandchildren. Just as important a story to them was that their eldest daughter, Esther, together with her husband, Reuben, and young family, was moving to Palestine.

Waiting for their passports had taken a few months, and in that time, David Blomberg arranged for them to rent rooms at an address he knew in Scheunenviertel, the main Jewish area of Berlin. He would have been pleased to join them, but as his wife was about to give birth to their second child, they would leave later on. Miriam was pleased to leave her job at the textile factory, and made tentative arrangements to buy merchandise to be sent to Berlin, if the prices were right and when they were ready to start up their business. It was an exciting, nerve-wracking, risky journey into the unknown, but they were young enough to take risks; they had worked and saved hard.

Finally, the day of their departure arrived, but their hope of joining a group did not happen. With Ezra and Shimon's help with their luggage, Jacub and Miriam boarded a tram to the main railway station to await their train for Berlin amid tears of sadness and promises to reunite in the not too distant future. Grandmother's decreasing mobility kept her at home, and Sara stayed with her, too upset at the thought of losing her family to Germany whose barbaric war was still fresh in her memory.

Chapter 2
Berlin

Scheunenviertel simultaneously shocked and, by reputation, did not shock Jacub and Miriam as they navigated their way through the small, narrow, dark streets to their accommodation, struggling with their cases past fruit and vegetable stalls on street corners, with restaurants and bakeries bearing the kosher sign, and more stalls selling milk, eggs and butter. A vibrant cacophony of varied sounds assaulted their ears... of traders raucously shouting their wares, blousy madams with keys jangling and clients in tow, theatre people, homosexuals and rent boys strutting their stuff, pimps and prostitutes interacting with clients, and furtive-looking petty criminals awaiting their chance to pick pockets, all strangely living alongside the ultra-Orthodox.

A contact of David Blomberg, a middle-aged Hasid named Abraham Hirsch, was busying himself at the address they had been given, and ushered them into a very modest room, plus kitchen, where the rent was fortuitously low and the noise pulsatingly loud. Below, Klezmer music infiltrated every corner of the buildings nearby. Abraham needed to be paid straight away in cash, and, after informing them of the rental terms, he disappeared down the rickety, dust-laden stairs into the street below.

It's all so desperately poverty-stricken, thought Miriam, as she perched on a well-worn chair after their long journey. She certainly didn't expect Berlin to be like this… it was a bit like the Baluty area of Lodz with scores of bearded, side-locked men in black, selling and bargaining as if their lives depended on it. And it was so crowded. It seemed as if dozens of different forms of humanity throbbed their lives away in murky, confined spaces. It was definitely not like arriving in the promised land. Jacub said nothing, his face a study of worried, thoughtful concentration.

When he finally spoke, it was to remind them both that the present accommodation was temporary, a place to stay while they organised their lives, and that they needed to learn a great deal in the next weeks as the basis for making sound decisions affecting their future livelihood. It seemed that the 'Golden Time' for Jews, and especially immigrant foreign Jews, was not nearly as positive as they had been led to believe in Lodz. Berlin had become an immigrant metropolis, and although the Ostjuden had fled to Germany to escape pogroms, violence and discrimination, Berlin public opinion was for 'unwelcome aliens', mostly unemployed, to be deported back to Poland or Russia. The German government had to pay unemployment benefits that following World War I they could ill afford, so therefore, the German army undertook manhunts in Berlin, expelling Jews from east of the city limits. Jacub and Miriam also learned that the President of the Reich Immigration Office had publicly stated that the Ostjuden were taking up the country's desperately needed work places. For Jews who intended to stay in Germany, work became a prerequisite for a residence permit. Therefore, residence permits would enable the immigrant to stay in Berlin without fear of deportation. It became clear to the couple that they should become self-employed.

In contacting some the small Jewish textile factories in Lodz, and even family and friends, deals could be made which could improve the lives of those living on both sides of the German/Polish border. Jacub set to work immediately, writing letters to those he knew in the trade, whilst Miriam followed the agreement made with her old boss in the factory where she had worked in Lodz. She and Jacub had also brought small amounts of merchandise with them which they priced with the help of Moshe, a brother of their landlord, Abraham Hirsch. They were determined to strive ahead to reach their goal without wasting any time, desperate to achieve success and a better life in this newly-adopted country. The fear of being rounded up by the army and expelled from Germany back to Poland was ever present on their minds.

In those first few days, Jacub and Miriam were caught up in a whirlwind of new experiences and ideologies. Their command of the German language was adequate to express what they needed in shops and business, but with the other Jewish immigrants they could relax into speaking the all-pervasive Yiddish. The Scheunenviertel area of Berlin, so Jewish and so poor, was teaming with immigrants from other nations, including those who had fled the Russian revolution, mostly White Russians who, it was rumoured, had brought their antisemitism with them. Through talking to their neighbours, Jacub realised that this area of Berlin had become a stopping place for many en route to America, Paris or London, but who had run out of money and needed to refill their coffers. For many it was simply a transitory place, and not one of permanency since it was so difficult to obtain residence permits.

The grim state of the tiny flat sickened Miriam who was fastidiously house proud, and she felt a powerful urge to sweep and scrub the dirty floors and walls and to sponge the meagre, dust-ridden furniture to an acceptable living standard. It was clear that the rent was based on space and not cleanliness. She would have liked to tell Abraham Hirsch where to put his grimy, shabby hovel of a flat and swan off to a pristine and comfortable hotel, but the rent was low, accommodation in short supply and they needed to save every zloty. It was the bed bugs which particularly distressed the couple. Poverty and dirt seemed to be inseparably united, so to disprove this thought, they spent their evenings grappling with hard soap, disinfectant, cloths and hot water heated on the primitive stove.

The lavatory, located in a dark corner on the stairwell, and shared by several families, was a very smelly place in which to spend as little time as possible, and needed drastic cleaning attention. Jacub and Miriam just hoped their cleaning efforts would inspire others to follow their example in the future.

Moshe Hirsch suggested that their merchandise could be sold from a stall in the Scheunenviertel market, and they managed to obtain more items from Miriam's old factory in Lodz at very encouraging prices which enabled them to make some money and settle the bill. Grandmother had sent them money to invest in their newly launched business, but she would not expect a future share in the profits. Jacub's eyes welled up with tears on reading her very brief letter. Jewish girls in her day had received very little education, but he knew that she would have saved and sacrificed over the years, and yet she always thought of others before herself.

Within weeks, after research into their retail possibilities, and with the help of Grandmother's gift, Jacub and Miriam were able to rent premises on Grosse Frankfurter Strasse, a cosmopolitan, poor Jewish area of crowded tenements, full of shops, cafés and delicatessens where people could stroll and window gaze, despite the poverty. The residents of that area formed a great left-wing stronghold who were constantly in conflict with fascist elements, and quite frequently riots and brawls were the outcome, though mainly after dark. Amusingly, the owner of this new acquisition, Samuel Lewinski, was a friend of Abraham Hirsch, and both had arrived in Berlin from Lodz shortly after the war in 1919. They had done well for themselves.

It was unlikely that Miriam and Jacub would ever rent premises further west in the city owing to the expense, and anyway, they felt secure in the camaraderie of other Jews in this area, particularly those from Lodz. So with their customary determined enthusiasm and keeping the dream of a better life as their guiding star, they cleaned and polished the shop again and again before preparing the front window with attractive items at tempting prices.

Satisfied with their progress, they locked up, and took a walk of exploration around the streets nearby, and those leading to another neighbourhood. They observed that not all Jews were poor. In fact, many were educated, cultured and wealthy. That was evident from where they lived and how they were dressed and were as unlike the Hasidim in Scheunenviertel as they could be. It was a well-known fact that German rabbis in the nineteenth century had advised their congregations to assimilate as far as possible into the German way of life, and thousands had chosen this route, disregarding orthodoxy, they became reformed Jews, proud to contribute to the great German culture, renowned throughout Europe. A significant number had made contributions in law, science, banking, theatre, music, medicine and trade. Having moved up the social hierarchy, many were irritated by the non-assimilation of the Hasidim.

Jacub researched additional sources of knitwear in both Berlin and Lodz so as to open the shop at the earliest date, not with a grand opening, but with attractive, affordable items and welcoming smiles. The advantage of Grosse Frankfurter Strasse, even though it was in a poor area, was that it was a long, densely populated and mainly Jewish street, full of life and vitality. Their first day of opening was encouraging, though not spectacular. They were making a little money, and, once a week, they had the added option of selling garments on the Scheunenviertel market, which might be more difficult to sell on Grosse Frankfurter Strasse.

As they worked hard to make a modest living and to settle into their new way of life, the months passed quickly. News from Jacub's parents in Lodz was undramatic on the whole. Ezra was now a member of the Jewish Socialist Workers' group, but the women folk, Sara and Grandmother, remained solidly supportive of Jacub and Miriam, regularly sending them examples of their work for sale in the Berlin shop. Shimon, on the other hand, had joined a yeshiva and, as young as he was, intent on devoting his life to the study of the Talmud and the Torah, to learn from history and to discover truth. He dressed in black now, had grown his sidelocks and wore a kippah all the time, much to the consternation of the secular Jews living in that part of Lodz.

When the Blombergs arrived in Berlin to settle in Scheunenviertel as near neighbours, Miriam particularly enjoyed the friendship of Rosa, with her new baby and young child, and the sharing of their Polish roots. Both the Blombergs and the Mendelsons, along with many others, had become fearful of what was happening to the German economy. It was as stagnant as that of Poland, if not worse. From reading the Yiddish newspaper, they became aware that the German government still owed millions in war reparations which they could not afford to pay, so French and Belgian soldiers had occupied the Ruhr to make certain that the debts were honoured by taking goods and raw materials in lieu of money. The German workers refused to cooperate and went on strike. To counter this problem, the German government had printed more and more banknotes which led to hyperinflation. The two families had seen long queues for food and the prices of everything rise since their arrival in the country, including the cost of bread, a basic commodity. Jacub and Miriam's own shop could not keep up with the extreme price rises. It was thought best to share ingredients to prepare communal meals two or three times a week for the two Lodz families.

Another serious worry was the street fights breaking out in Scheunenviertel between mainly Communist Jews from the East and German right-wing factions. The latter targeted the Ostjuden so that violence became a regular occurrence in the Weimar Republic, with painful consequences. Hyperinflation, it seemed, devalued both money and human life.

The undercurrent of antisemitism in German society broke out forcefully in November 1923, following the regular distribution of antisemitic posters and pamphlets. With tears in her eyes, Miriam read one aloud.

"How much longer do you want to be treated like foreigners in your own city? How much longer will you accept thousands of Polish and Russian Jews arriving and taking your homes, your food and the clothes off your back?"

As the year progressed, trade in the shop slowed down to a virtual standstill. Potential customers simply could not afford to buy, so Jacub and Miriam used their stall in the market instead and temporarily closed the shutters of their shop, in the hope of increasing their sales on the street, like so many others. Scores of hawkers, dishevelled and tramp-like, occupied the streets of Scheunenviertel. Many were

Ostjuden, but others were war veterans, the disabled and the unemployed, all trying to beat hyperinflation, intent on earning their next meal. The shopkeepers were livid, claiming that hawkers put them at a gross disadvantage commercially.

Furiously, one of them attacked a Jewish hawker, and before long things escalated into a full-scale riot, spreading rapidly throughout the area in an incredibly vicious way. It was as if all hell had been let loose after a long period of repressed resentment. With hundreds of others, Jacub and Miriam fled for home, as crowds smashed shop windows with clubs and looted the contents, leaving evidence of shards of glass and vandalism on the pavements. In relief and fear they were thankful that they had closed the shutters of their shop, and they peered out from behind the curtains of the flat at the continuing riot below, noticing that the police had arrived, were firing into the air in order to disperse the warring crowd, and patrolled with rifles, batons and bayonets whilst fires smouldered in buildings close by.

Miriam secretly wondered if they had made a serious mistake in coming to Berlin since they had not witnessed anything as violent or destructive in Lodz, but she decided not to share her thoughts with Jacub, at least not for the moment.

The following days revealed that two people had died and over forty had been injured in the riot. The police, who were of the opinion that the violence was due to the criminal excesses of the rabble rather than to antisemitism, arrested five hundred and seventy-one people for looting, and concluded that trade had shifted from the shops to the streets, with hundreds of hawkers competing with each other for the best spaces.

The Zionist newspaper 'Judische Rundschau' claimed the riot to be a pogrom perpetrated by an antisemitic mob, whereas right-wing newspapers accused foreign Jews of taking advantage of an economic crisis, and of antagonising the unemployed with 'dirty' street trade. Most newspapers claimed that right-wing, racist agitators had instigated and stoked the riot. Jacub, Miriam and their friends David and Rosa Blomberg were very shaken up by the whole experience, and were in fear of another similar riot breaking out in the future, their top priority being safety. David was a landlord of four small flats in a nearby tenement, and therefore was not involved in trade or running a shop, but both he and Jacub thought it best not to return to the shop on Grosse Frankfurter Strasse until the situation had quietened down.

This unstable political situation was resolved when Gustav Stresemann as German Chancellor, and supported by the Social Democrats, negotiated with the USA regarding the problems of hyperinflation. Charles G. Dawes, an American banker, recommended a plan which became known as the Dawes Plan. Germany would pay less money in reparations every year to make the payments easier. In addition, the USA would lend Germany money to help put the country back on its feet. Charles Dawes advised using a new currency known as the Rentenmark which was based on the value of all German land and assets. By limiting the amount of credit and money in circulation, the economy was brought under control... at least temporarily.

Life was gradually eased for the German population, and the Mendelsons applied themselves assiduously to making a success of their knitwear shop, even though Grosse Frankfurter Strasse was in a poor area, by passing on the current needs and styles of new fashion within an affordable range to their sources of supply.

Chapter 3
Changes

The Golden Age shone for Germany and for the immigrant Ostjuden in the latter half of the 1920s, thanks to America and the Dawes Plan. More than twenty-five billion dollars were injected into the moribund German economy which, combined with financial and industrial expertise, brought about a surge in production. The French and Belgians withdrew from the Ruhr, and between 1925 and 1928 prosperity was restored.

Jacub and Miriam felt the positive effects of prosperity in their shop; more money was in circulation and therefore more items were being bought. Prices had stabilised, and Berlin residents, including the Ostjuden, were enjoying an improved standard of living, although poverty was by no means eliminated. The Mendelsons were able to save a little for their future, and as they did so they started to think about a residence permit. Gone were the days when they had secretly wished to return to Lodz. They felt that now their future in Germany was assured.

In the summer of 1925, Rosa announced that she was expecting her third child and Miriam, instead of feeling sad and jealous, was delighted because wonder of wonders she, too, had missed her woman's time, felt nauseous in the mornings, and later she noticed her waistline

37

thickening. At first, she was unsure, and did not tell Jacub, but when she became certain, she blurted out the news to him, and after all the years of waiting and disappointment, he could scarcely believe it, having become philosophical about the problem, leaving it in God's hands. He just sat down, holding her to him, and he cried. They both cried with joy and gratitude, realising that all their past pain was just a memory, and were eager to share their delight with David and Rosa who were old hands at this parenting business. The two children would be born within weeks of each other. Jacub, fearful of the pregnancy not reaching full term, became very protective of Miriam, insisting that she rest in the afternoons whilst he remained in the shop, which she didn't appreciate at all mainly because, as she pointed out to Jacub, their tiny, shabby, unlovable flat was always considered very temporary, and not fit for their new baby. She would much rather spend the time looking for a larger flat in a less troubled area.

As the shop was proving moderately successful, and there was clearly more money around in Berlin, enabling them to save for difficult times and providing them with a modicum of security, elusive to them in the early years, Jacub agreed that now was the time to move and prepare a new home for their long-awaited baby. Both Abraham and Moshe Hirsch helped with the search which ended successfully with the acquisition of a two-bedroomed flat in Friedenstrasse, and a fair rent was negotiated. It was situated in a working-class area of tenements and left-wing residents, mainly Social Democrats and Communists, Jews and non-Jews, and close to the Volkspark; in fact, the park could be seen from their windows.

They withdrew from their present accommodation, having given a month's notice, and were overjoyed to move into their new home. This flat was unfurnished, so a bed, table and chairs became immediate necessities. None of the items was new, but as Jacub and Miriam gradually acquired second-hand pieces of furniture, they were able to clean and polish them to their satisfaction. What would become the baby's room was scrubbed and painted white.

To celebrate the good news about the forthcoming babies, Jacub and Miriam decided to spend a weekend in Wannsee with David, Rosa and their family. The lake was beautiful, the children would be able to play on the beach in the sunshine and they could all enjoy relaxation and fun for a short time before getting back to work, and in Jacub's case, back to the shop. Wannsee was only a short train ride, whereas a Baltic seaside resort would mean a journey of about two hundred kilometres. They arrived early at a moderately priced hotel in the hope of reserving rooms for the weekend to be told that Jewish guests were not welcome. It was a quite flagrant, unexpected piece of antisemitism, and they were aghast. Rosa started to cry quietly, and then her little girls caught the atmosphere and began to wail and sob. While Miriam and Jacub helped pacify the children, David, made of sterner stuff, entered the next hotel to make a similar reservation. He received an almost identical reply. The hotel was full, (although it clearly wasn't) and it was not their policy to accommodate Jews. It would be unbearable to receive that rejection a third time, so they all decided to spend the whole day on the beach and then return to Friedenstrasse in the evening. They did not concern themselves with holidays again.

In their daily lives, what became unnerving, despite increased prosperity, were the frequent fights breaking out in Scheunenviertel between left-wing agitators and communists, many of whom were Jewish, and right-wing radicals. Antisemitic insults were bandied about as if they had become an accepted part of the German language, and the Ostjuden, especially the Hasidim, remained a target for regular bullying by right-wing radicals. A party calling themselves National Socialists had emerged whose leader, an Austrian, was called Adolf Hitler, and it was well-known that their twenty five-point Nazi manifesto included an antisemitic paragraph, and nobody seemed to be objecting to it.

Rosa and Miriam both needed to have their pregnancies monitored at the Jewish Hospital in Berlin, the… Krankenhaus der Judischen Gemeinde in Heinz-Galinski Strasse. Miriam was particularly grateful to have a friend in Rosa who told her about what preparations to make, what to expect, what to buy and generally provided her with moral support. Miriam would not buy anything for the baby in case disaster struck, nor would she allow Jacub to pass on the good news to his parents until a good few months had passed, but it was such a relief to her to feel normal like everyone else and to be liberated from the hints and expectation that had been so much part of her life in Lodz. To repay Rosa's kindness, she looked after her little girls sometimes or collected them from kindergarten. Occasionally, they would take a picnic into the Volkspark on a sunny day, although Miriam did not shirk her duties at the shop. There was regular paper work to be done in connection with orders and stock, unpacking, window dressing and pricing. In fact, she started to feel very tired and needed to rest after the shop closed and the evening meal was served.

Berlin winters tended to be very cold and the one leading into 1926 was no exception. Snow fell thick, and bitter winds blew in from the Urals. Knitwear was certainly popular, and Jacub extended their range in gloves, socks, scarfs, pullovers and woolly hats, which sold particularly well. Even so, when March arrived with its presage of spring, everyone, it seemed, was relieved. Miriam, then in her seventh month of pregnancy, had been forced to be very wary of frozen surfaces, and longed for the time when she would hold her baby in her arms.

The last two months passed slowly, and when Rosa gave birth to her third child, a boy they named Samuel, there was great rejoicing at the New Synagogue where relatives and friends gathered for the Brit Milar, or circumcision. Miriam started to feel anxious about the future. Rosa seemed to have taken everything in her stride with an almost problem-free pregnancy and a rapid delivery. Her own birthing experience, however, was the opposite. What she dreaded came true. The labour was long and painful, and so exhausting that a caesarean section became necessary not only for her but also for the survival of the baby. When she awoke from the anaesthetic, Jacub was smiling, with tears pouring down his face, as she was given a precious bundle... a beautiful baby boy. They named him Josef, and as Miriam gazed down at him, despite her exhaustion and loss of blood, she felt a powerful surge of love for this tiny child and… that she would do everything in her power to protect him from harm.

Thrilled by the arrival of their grandson, Ezra and Sarah travelled to Berlin to see him and to offer their support. They stayed with Jacub at Friedenstrasse bringing with them a host of baby clothes and baby gifts, including a pram. Since Miriam was still in a weak, post-operative state, the Brit Milar was performed at the Jewish Hospital in the company of family and friends, a joyful time for them all. Sadly, the doctor who performed the caesarean, broke the news to the couple that Miriam would not be able to give birth again, so their joy was tinged with sadness, as Josef would remain an only child. According to Jewish custom, and when her health improved, Miriam went to the mikvah (ritual pool) to cleanse herself after having given birth.

The news from Lodz was mixed. Grandmother was quite well considering her age and was assiduously working on the loom. She hoped that Jacub and Miriam would visit Lodz soon so that she could pamper her one and only great grandson. Shimon, Jacub's brother, was still dedicated to Hasidism, but, together with another friend, had been beaten up by a group of thugs on his way home from the yeshiva in the evening. Their distinctive clothing rendered them easy targets. Fortunately, no bones were broken, just cuts and several painful bruises. The most surprising piece of news was that Miriam's sister, Esther, with husband Reuben and family had returned from Palestine. Their business prospects had not materialised, and they were homesick for family and friends. Life, back in Lodz, was difficult while they searched for work once more, but at least they were reunited with family.

Eventually Ezra and Sarah returned to Lodz after spending a few weeks in Berlin, and life returned to normal. Miriam breastfed Josef which kept her close to home at first, but once her routine was established, she and Rosa and a new friend, Margrethe, together with their progeny, would often join each other for walks in the park, for a little shopping or for just being together. Relatively tranquil months passed and turned into years. The children were taken to a Jewish kindergarten together where they did not feel strange, and Miriam was able to spend a few hours helping Jacub with the shop. For reasons of security he did not like to leave her alone there, so she was often able to collect Josef from kindergarten and bring him to their shop to see his father. Business continued to be satisfactory, and they kept well in touch with their suppliers, particularly those in Lodz.

It soon became clear to his doting parents that Josef was a bright, alert child. He was forever asking questions, wanting to make things out of scraps, to be kept occupied and, above all, eager to learn to read. On Jacub's return from the shop in the evening, Josef would ask his father to teach him; he would sit on his lap and soak up all the information he could whilst Miriam was preparing the evening meal. The couple were bilingual in Yiddish and Polish, but their command of German was only average.

Having been born in Berlin, Josef was German by nationality and would attend a German school, so his basic reading books had to be in German. He loved the pictures and wanted to read the messages under them. Jacub, himself, had always enjoyed books when given the time, and treated these daily reading sessions with his son as precious. It also gave him a chance to improve his own grasp of the language, and above all, both he and Miriam were anxious to do the very best for Josef, particularly as he would have no brothers or sisters.

As secular Jews, Miriam and Jacub were in favour of assimilating into the German way of life, much like thousands of others, and therefore decided to enrol Josef into a local state school when the time came. After kindergarten, German formal education began at age six to seven and as Josef was a bright child, he started the volksschule in 1932 when he was six years old, and already well able to read. A year later, David and Rosa's boy, Samuel, started to attend the Jewish school on Grosse Hamburger Strasse.

Chapter 4
The Economic Collapse of Germany and the Rise of Adolf Hitler

From 1924 onwards, thanks to the Dawes Plan and massive American investment to build up the economy, Germany flourished artificially with prosperity and production until 1929 when the Wall Street Crash occurred, causing dire economic problems and mass unemployment in the USA. Other countries were severely affected too, and particularly Germany whose financial wellbeing was based on loans.

America was effectively bankrupt by the end of 1929 and consequently gave Germany ninety days to start to repay the money loaned to her. Great Britain and France were disinclined and unable to inject money into the German economy since they were also seriously affected by the Crash and by World War I.

Throughout Germany, fifty thousand companies went bankrupt, particularly in industrial areas, agricultural prices fell and workers were laid off in their millions. Most of the unemployed were family men, who became unable to supply food, a home, heating or clothes to their dependants. The majority of families were affected in one way or another; some were literally starving whilst others lost their homes through not paying the rent, and had to pitch tents in public parks or allotments. By 1932 six million were unemployed. Five major banks folded, and savings were lost. The people were desperate about the failures of the Weimar Republic and wanted change with strong leadership so that they could regain their jobs. Nazism and Communism promised solutions to Germany's economic and social problems. In Friedenstrasse, the neighbours of the Mendelsons were either pro Communist or Social Democrat.

Emergency unemployment payments were low, and in some cases, workers received nothing at all. The good old spending days of 1924 to 1928 were over, and in their shop on Grosse Frankfurter Strasse, Jacub and Miriam experienced very poor trade indeed as Berliners were concerned more with feeding themselves than buying new clothes. In the Volkspark they noticed rows of tents being erected for needy families, and soup kitchens attracting scores of undernourished children. In his first weeks at school in 1932, Josef's class included a number of impoverished pupils, some tough-looking, others pale and lethargic, with poor clothes and grubby appearance. In the streets, antisemitic comments were flung around openly without inhibition, and it was fortunate for young Josef that his fairish hair and grey eyes were not obviously Jewish features.

Jacub hoped that he would not be forced to go to the Jewish Welfare agencies in Berlin which were maintained by congregational giving at the synagogues, and through donations, endowments and bequests from wealthy Jewish members of Berlin society. David Blomberg's tenants were unable to pay their rent which meant an end to his livelihood or their eviction, so a visit to their rabbi and the Jewish Welfare office would hopefully produce a solution. Miriam helped out at the Jewish soup kitchens whilst Josef was at school, and she was proud to know how well he was doing there. Most days he returned home with all the news of what he was learning, and of more dramatic events of children fainting through hunger whilst on the school premises. Finally, Jacub was forced to go to the Jewish Welfare office, having spent all their savings and Grandmother's money on maintaining the two rents, terrified about being evicted from their home, and from their livelihood, the shop.

The economic situation nationally became so serious in 1933 that President von Hindenburg appointed Adolf Hitler as Chancellor, with the Nazi party being part of a coalition government. With such economic instability and poverty, the German population became receptive to the words and promises of the Nazi party which had been growing in strength for several years, and particularly to the rhetoric of their leader, Adolf Hitler, a powerful and charismatic orator. At the time of the 1932 elections, the Nazis became the largest party in the Reichstag (German Parliament) yet without a majority. The Sturmabteilung or SA, known as the Brownshirts or Storm Troopers, numbered four hundred thousand by 1932, many of whom were ruffians and bullies. They disrupted the political meetings of Nazis' opponents, created havoc against Communists and Socialists on the streets, and protected Hitler at his own meetings.

The Germans who opposed National Socialism failed

to unite against it, and the conservatives in the parliamentary coalition virtually gave the Nazis the power they demanded. When Hitler seized power in January 1933, he quickly passed an 'Enabling Law' which gave the party power to promulgate laws without parliamentary approval. The act allowed Hitler and his cabinet to rule by emergency decree for four years, although Hindenburg remained president. The emergency rule quickly turned into dictatorship.

Following the Reichstag fire in February 1933, perpetrated by a group of communists, Hitler immediately set about abolishing the powers of the individual German states and the existence of non-Nazi political parties and organisations... in fact, democracy. He suspended basic rights, controlled the police and allowed arrest without trial, which led to the mass arrests of communists, and this was combined with vitriolic anti-communist propaganda. Social Democrats were detained and physically intimidated. In the first week of this dictatorship, over twenty anti-fascists were killed by the Nazi para-military during political brawls, several socialist and communist newspapers were banned, telephones were tapped and letters intercepted. Captain Hermann Goering forced the police into shooting anyone who showed the slightest opposition. When President von Hindenburg died in August 1934, Hitler combined the offices of President and Chancellor for himself, with no chance of him being dismissed, and on that day all soldiers took the Hitler Oath swearing unconditional obedience to the Commander-in-Chief, Adolf Hitler.

Chapter 5
Troubles

Jacub read out the antisemitic paragraph in the twenty five-point Nazi Plan which dated back to 1920, and which he had known about for a number of years.

No-one who is not of a German race should be allowed to live in Germany. Those who started living in Germany after August 1914 should leave the country. Only Germans can be citizens. No Jew can be a German citizen.

Jacub thought about all the loyal Jews who had served Germany for generations, for centuries even, and in many cases considered themselves more German than Jewish, but now were not permitted to be German citizens. Surely not. He and Miriam were Polish Jews, hoping to gain residence permits, but what about all those who had been born in Germany, (like their son Josef) and had pledged allegiance and service to the country? Thousands of Jews had fought and died for their country in the Great War, and now the survivors were to be denied their citizenship? It was unthinkable. He was sure it would not happen. That part of the manifesto would be revoked, he was certain, and he looked forward to better times, keeping a positive attitude and advising Miriam to do the same. Whereas Miriam agreed to maintain optimism for the sake of Josef, she was quietly more realistic about a worsening situation than was her husband and wondered what other antisemitic horrors lay in store for the Jewish community in the future.

She had but a short time to wait. On Saturday 1ˢᵗ April, the diminutive Joseph Goebbels, parading the streets of Berlin with the benefit of loudspeakers, and surrounded by hundreds of members of the Sturmabteilung Brown Shirts, repeated in diverse neighbourhoods the following:

"Germans, defend yourselves against the Jewish atrocity propaganda. Buy only at German shops. Don't buy from Jews!"

The timing of this exercise was ill-considered since most Jews closed their shops on the Sabbath, keeping off the streets and out of trouble, but after the weekend, a large star of David in white paint adorned the shutters of the Mendelsons' shop, and scores of others. Many other shopkeepers on Grosse Frankfurter Strasse were Jewish anyway, as were the vast majority of their customers.

David Blomberg called round to see the family one evening in May (1933), bringing Samuel with him so as to meet up with Josef, since they attended different schools. The boys, now known as Sam and Joe to both parents and friends, often played in the Volkspark with other boys of similar age, although those friends never included non-Jewish boys now. David seemed rather shaken up and nervous which surprised Jacub, knowing him to be a resourceful, confident and positive character. He explained that out of curiosity he had attended a speech from Joseph Goebbels. In the fervent, hate-filled diatribe, Goebbels claimed that Jewish intellectualism was dead. Following the speech to a crowd of forty thousand, members of the

German Student Union burned more than twenty-five thousand volumes of un-German books in the Opernplatz, the square of the State Opera House in Berlin. The books were regarded as subversive or containing ideologies opposed to Nazism, mainly Jewish, and would never again be found in libraries, schools or universities. David, was recognised as Jewish by members of the crowd, and several yelled out, "Dirty Jew," as he hurried away to avoid trouble.

"I'm really worried about our future." His voice broke with emotion. "And in the short term, it's even dangerous to go out. Scores of Jews were rounded up after that meeting to be sent off to prison who knows where, and for doing nothing wrong. I was nearly caught myself. Just for being Jewish, it seems, and there are hate posters everywhere. Whatever you do, make sure you are not a member of any political party. Give them no excuse for arresting you and keep a low profile. Women seem to be less threatened on the streets than men."

That was good advice indeed. Jacub knew of communists and Social Democrats in their building and in the tenements nearby who were actively involved in politics and had engaged in brawls with Nazis on several occasions in the past, but now that they were in power, brawls were the least of it. He and Miriam would have nothing to do with politics; they would concentrate on their son and their livelihood at the shop. Attempting to make life more equal through political means was out of the question in this dictatorship.

A few weeks after this episode, a group of communists

in Friedenstrasse were rounded up by the SA at night and sent off to Dachau, the first concentration camp.

The death of President von Hindenburg came and went in 1934, inciting Adolph Hitler into perpetrating further, flagrant penalties against the Jews. The entire civil service was now devoid of their employment. Jewish doctors could no longer treat non-Jewish patients, and Jewish teachers were no longer permitted to work in German state schools. Joe had noticed the absence of one of his own teachers, Frau Frankel, and was sad to know the reason. She had always been kind, and he had responded to her clear instruction and encouragement. Not long after she had told Miriam that Joe was clearly an academic child, a delight to teach and destined for the gymnasium, she was relieved of her position at the school. Fortunately for Joe, there were two other Jewish boys in his class, Heinrich Rosenbaum and Chaim Goldstein.

It wasn't simply the absence of Frau Frankel that had changed in the school. Other Jewish teachers had been dismissed too, but there were extra, noticeable changes. A picture of Adolf Hitler could be found in every classroom, and the pupils were expected to raise their arms in the 'Heil Hitler' salutation position with great enthusiasm, always at the start of the day, sometimes at the beginning of each lesson and out of school too, should they meet a member of staff. Many teachers wore their Nazi uniform, some were very involved with the Hitler Youth, and the teacher who had replaced Frau Frankel was of questionable teaching ability. The pupils were not expected to wear a uniform except on 20th April, Hitler's birthday. As Jews,

Joe, Heinrich and Chaim were not eligible to join the Hitler Youth, which made them feel very left out, as it was intended to do, knowing that their classmates would be enjoying sports, rambles and camping after school and at the weekends, and that all Jewish Youth movements had been banned.

"I don't want to be Jewish," moaned Joe to his mother one day on his return from school. "It's so unfair. We can't do any exciting stuff that our classmates do in the Hitler Youth like sports and camping, and we even get left out of school trips. It's because we're Jewish. And in lesson time we're sent to the back of the class as if we're not really part of the class at all."

He burst into tears, and for a short time was inconsolable. When he had calmed down, Miriam took him in her arms and explained that she and Jacub were proud of their Jewish heritage, and that he should be too, that Jews had suffered for various reasons over the centuries and that it was a bad time for Jews in Germany at the moment. The bad times would hopefully pass, and he must stay strong. As he got older, he could study Jewish history, and be proud of their heroes, prophets and achievements, but for now some activities organised at the New Synagogue with Heinrich, Chaim and Sam might be a good idea. Joe took heart from his mother's words, but it would not be the only time that he would shed tears for the worsening situation in Germany.

A few weeks later, Heinrich announced to Joe and Chaim whilst in the yard at school that he and his family would be leaving Berlin to go and live in Paris.

"My father is a lawyer, and he's lost his job, so he doesn't want to stay in Germany anymore. He and my mother can speak French, and we have relatives in Paris, so we'll be leaving as soon as we can."

Joe was sad and Chaim said nothing, but after school older boys from a class above, who had been informed that Heinrich would be leaving, taunted him.

"When are you leaving, dirty Jew? That's one less. Come here and we'll give you a good hiding before you leave. Death to all the Jews!" Then they burst into laughter.

The three younger boys ran back into school to report what had happened, but received no support from the member of staff. She was not interested.

As the months passed, several Jewish children in other classes at the school failed to turn up for their lessons, and after some time, it was assumed that they had left the country.

Due to the risk of Jacub being rounded up, the Mendelsons determined to go out regularly as a family in an obviously Jewish area, rather than in a politically provocative one or at night, for even without a curfew it could be dangerous on the streets with the SA itching to humiliate or beat up Jews. Playing games with other Jewish children on a Sunday in the Volkspark became a regular occurrence which the parents could enjoy too. Miriam liked to shop for groceries with Rosa for company whilst Jacub was at work, and they discovered together that the kosher butcher had closed down, gone out of business, forcing them to patronise a German butcher if they wanted to eat meat. Margarethe, their other friend, had left Berlin with her husband and two children to move to Amsterdam to remove themselves from Nazi tyranny. It was obvious that the miserable, restrictive practices imposed on the Jews were inciting thousands to leave the country which is exactly what the Nazis wanted.

Many elderly Jewish people could be seen on the streets looking hapless and alone, as if the younger members of their families had taken flight, and Jacub already knew of a couple in their sixties living in a nearby tenement in Friedenstrasse who had taken their own lives... a fact he kept from Joe who was facing almost daily challenges of antisemitic abuse at school. Chaim looked more obviously Jewish than Joe, but since the Nazi curriculum attached great importance to race and racial characteristics, the teacher requested the boys to stand in front of the class whilst the pupils studied their physiognomies and type, the object of the lesson being to prove that Jews were Untermenschen or inferior. It was humiliating for them, and the only way for them to take their revenge was to shine academically with their hard work and brains. The bullies were shown to be dull and stupid which unfortunately only increased their anger and abuse. Both Jacub and Miriam wanted Joe to learn how to stand up for himself in what was often a cruel and violent world, but he was a sensitive, thoughtful boy and sometimes it became necessary to meet him and Chaim from school.

More vicious antisemitic laws were promulgated in September 1935 at Nuremberg where there had been mass meetings of the Nazi hierarchy and tens of thousands of adoring disciples, hanging onto Hitler's every evil word. Miriam read in the Berliner Tagblatt that these laws excluded all Jews from Reich citizenship, and that their passports would need a large, red J for Jew stamped on them. She also read that marriages or sexual contact between Germans and Jews were now banned in order to protect the German race from contamination. Well, that law would affect them not at all, but as she read on down the column, she noticed that Jews were no longer allowed in swimming pools, theatres, restaurants or parks. This was a terrible blow. What were they to do with Joe, Chaim and Sam in the free time after school or at the weekend? Why was this happening? She felt overwhelmed by the sheer hatred of the government in power, and by the generally poisoned atmosphere in the city. She was on her own in the flat, and she cried uncontrollably for many minutes, releasing anger and fear which had built up inside her. Then she dried her eyes and applied some make-up so that Jacub and Joe would not notice.

The New Synagogue on Oranienburger Strasse, built in 1866, was the main synagogue of the Berlin Jewish Community, a beautiful building in the Moorish style of architecture and able to seat over three thousand worshippers. It was especially frequented by the immigrants from the East. David Blomberg and family attended shul regularly, and the rabbi agreed that Sam and Joe could learn Hebrew there once a week, along with a group of boys, even though they were both too young to make their Bar Mitzvah. There would also be games and refreshments afterwards as a reward for the study. Joe was excited about this suggestion and hoped that Chaim would join the group too. It certainly compensated a little for not being able to play in the park or go to the swimming pool, and they would be free from humiliation and bullying. The building housed public concerts, too, in aid of poor Jews who had been excluded from government benefits, which the Mendelsons and Blombergs attended and supported.

When Joe invited Chaim the next day to join him at the synagogue, he could scarcely believe the news that he and his family would be leaving as soon as possible for Belgium. His only friend in the school would be gone, and he would be the only Jewish boy left in the class. His heart was full of sadness, and he cried.

"You're on your own now, little Jew boy," jeered the usual bullies in the yard the next day after lesson time, although they stopped short when they saw Jacub meeting his son at the school gate.

Jacub saw and heard the bullies, strapping and oaf-like, and knew that action needed to be taken. The decision to assimilate and to send Joe to a Berlin state school had failed dismally, and both parents agreed not to prolong his pain and loneliness. With this in mind, they approached the headteacher of the Jewish Boys' School, the Judische Freyschule, in Grosse Hamburger Strasse in the hope that Joe would gain a place, knowing that his friend, Sam Blomberg, was already a pupil there.

Chapter 6
Serious Developments

Joe was fortunate to be granted a place in the Jewish Boys' school with its crowded classrooms. Although many Jewish children had moved abroad with their parents to free themselves from an oppressive Nazi tyranny, hundreds more who were unable to leave the country had also experienced regular bullying and racial abuse in the state schools until life became unbearable for them. To be accepted by a Jewish school was often akin to being released from a nightmare, and unfortunately, many children were forced to remain in the state schools until 1938.

For Joe it was both a change and a relief. The atmosphere was welcoming, and stimulated interest in his heritage, and in Hebrew, as well as in academic subjects. He felt secure in the knowledge that he was among his own people who wished him well, and even if they argued often, they would never humiliate or bully him. He just wished that his parents had chosen this school when he was six instead of sending him to the German state school. It was clear that many other parents had made the same decision for reasons of assimilation. For the first time, he was proud of being Jewish and it felt good. He wasn't in the same class as Sam Blomberg, but he met him in the corridors sometimes and in their free time. In his own class the boys worked hard and asked questions. He enjoyed the achievement, camaraderie and humour which had certainly been lacking in the state school.

Sometimes on leaving school at the end of classes, a gang of bullies, very often from the Hitler Youth, would pounce on the Jewish boys and beat them up. The Jewish staff were aware of this and often broke up the fighting which, Joe remembered, the Nazi teachers had failed to do. However, away from the school surroundings and on their way home, Jewish boys would frequently be set upon by the Hitler Youth who were never on their own, always in a group. (Single members did not fight, and on the whole, Jewish girls were not attacked.) Sometimes they sang Nazi songs about Jewish blood flowing, and then laughed heartily.

Joe thrived at the Jewish school in Grosse Hamburger Strasse, made more friends, performed well academically and was able to enjoy the games the school offered as well as the weekly Hebrew classes at the synagogue. Miriam and Jacub noticed the improvement in Joe's morale and were relieved that he had now accepted Judaism with pride.

The year 1936 was in part an easier year for Jews owing to the Olympic Games held in Berlin and Garmisch-Partenkirchen. Hitler had been rather anxious that many countries would boycott Germany due to the persecution of the Jews, and consequently transfer the Games to another country which would have been a great blow to German prestige, international tourism and revenue. With this in mind, the Nazi party toned down its antisemitic activities and rhetoric, and removed signs saying "Jews Unwelcome" from public places. Joe, his family and friends were able to return to the Volkspark for picnics, games and relaxation at least for a short time. The Jewish community were in no way fooled that these actions represented a softening attitude to them in the future. It was simply a public relations exercise to achieve what the regime wanted in the short term. Of course, the children hoped that everything would improve for them in the future, but their parents were less optimistic.

As soon as the Olympic Games ended, the antisemitic signs returned, in fact increased, and the persecution of the Jews took an outrageous turn for the worse. A decree from the Reich Propaganda Ministry forbade Jewish soldiers being named among the dead in World War I memorials when they had given their lives for their country. Just like all the previous regulations, this one reinforced the message that Jews were outsiders whether they had been born in Germany or not.

So many Jews had lost their employment from the first round of restrictions in 1933; civil servants, lawyers, teachers and doctors, preventing them from earning a living. Now the economic exclusion began to develop further. They were required to register all their property both domestic and foreign, together with their assets. This would later lead to a gradual expropriation of their property by the State. Jacub and Miriam did not possess property either in Berlin or in Poland, paying rent on both the shop and the flat, so the new legislation did not apply to them. David Blomberg, however, owned four small flats which he rented out, and therefore had to divulge the addresses of all of them. He became rather nervous about the situation and wondered if more taxes were to be levied against the Jews.

The next piece of Nazi legislation involved the 'aryanisation' of Jewish businesses. Jewish managers and their workers were dismissed, and their companies were transferred to non-Jewish Germans who bought them at prices well below the market value. The money arising went to the State. In this way, thousands more Jews found themselves out of work and unable to provide for their families. The number of suicides continued to rise. Those Jews who could, arranged to leave as soon as possible... to Great Britain, Palestine, France, Belgium, Holland, South America, the United States and some as far away as China... but there were still thousands left, many of whom were elderly.

The Nazis had no intention of allowing refugees to take anything of material value out of the country, and so Jews were forced to leave their homes and businesses behind them which were then purloined by the State. They were also subject to heavy emigration taxes. The German authorities restricted the amount of money which could be transferred abroad and allowed each passenger to take only ten Reichsmarks out of the country. In consequence, most German Jews who managed to emigrate were totally impoverished by the time they reached their host countries. None of this applied to the Mendelsons who had no plans to move. In spite of SA thugs who tried to prevent clients from patronising their shop from time to time, Jacub and Miriam continued to make a very modest living selling knitwear to mainly Jewish customers. And yet would aryanisation raise its ugly head at their shop? The owner was Jewish, so logically a non-Jew could take it over and dismiss Jacub and Miriam from their livelihood. So far that had happened only on a grander scale, but the possibility filled them with worry and fear.

To try to emigrate to another country was a lengthy business requiring red tape; money for tickets, visas and emigration tax which the Mendelsons did not have. The aryanisation continued, and they knew that sooner or later they would be affected. The added problem was that countries which had accepted refugees in the earlier Nazi years had now reached their quotas and would accept no more. Quite a bit of time at Joe's school was spent preparing the pupils for emigration in spite of this. It seemed that tens of thousands were planning to leave for South America, and about eighteen thousand for Shanghai and Manchuria. Those who hoped that conditions would improve in Germany and who had neither the means nor the stomach for uprooting themselves were mainly the elderly. Among this group suicides occurred frequently.

Events continued to unfold rapidly in 1938, which was considered to be the fateful year.

The Anschluss, or the annexation of Austria, took place in March 1938 which incited even more Austrian Jews to want to emigrate. The Hitler Youth forced many eminent Jews to clean the streets of Vienna and elsewhere, whilst the Nazis deprived them of their assets. More concentration camps were opened: Sachsenhausen and Buchenwald in Germany, Mauthausen in Austria. The beating up of Jews on the streets increased and was followed by their transport to a concentration camp. Jacub had to be very watchful and cautious about his movements in Berlin. It was often, in fact, dangerous to go out; he and Miriam were sick with worry.

The Gestapo had been formed by Hermann Goering in 1933, and by 1938 it was under the jurisdiction of Heinrich Himmler. Foreign Jews in Germany were the first to suffer Nazi persecution as a specific group, and in October 1938, seventeen thousand Jews of Polish citizenship, many of whom had been living in Germany for decades, were arrested and relocated across the Polish border. Since the Polish government refused to admit them, they were interned indefinitely in 'relocation camps', a sort of no man's land between Germany and Poland.

On 19th October, two Gestapo agents arrested Jacub in his home at 77 Friedenstrasse and deported him to Poland, allowing him to take only his coat, hat and passport. Fortunately for him, his passport was up to date, enabling him to go directly to his family in Lodz and not to a relocation camp like thousands of his compatriots. In the room next door, his son, Joe, was trembling with fear and pretended to be asleep, unable to say goodbye to his father. Miriam was told that she and Joe were allowed to stay in Berlin temporarily until they had officially organised their departure. When the Gestapo left, she and Joe broke down and wept. So much injustice and suffering had been the lot of their friends and acquaintances over the last few years, but it was the first time that the Mendelsons had been so painfully affected as a family.

German Jews would suffer yet again, this time from an event in France which happened within a few weeks of Jacub's expulsion from Berlin. On 7th November a seventeen-year-old Polish Jew named Herschel Grynspan walked into the German Embassy in Paris and shot a minor diplomat, Ernst von Rath. The young man did not resist arrest, and while in custody he told the authorities that he had shot von Rath as an act of revenge for the expulsion of Polish Jews from Germany weeks before. His parents, like thousands of other Jews, were forced to live in a refugee camp in Zbaszyn near the Polish border after they were denied entry into Poland.

The murder was the perfect excuse for the Nazis to escalate their campaign of hatred against the Jews. The propaganda minister, Joseph Goebbels, gave a speech indicating that the Nazis would not prevent any 'spontaneous' protests against the Jews who collectively were blamed for the murder. Thus, all over Germany and certainly in Berlin, on 9th and 10th November, Nazis were whipped into a frenzy of violence against the Jews. Thousands of homes and businesses were destroyed and the contents looted, two hundred and sixty-seven synagogues were also looted and set on fire. At least ninety-one Jews were killed and about thirty thousand Jewish men were arrested and sent off to concentration camps. The New Synagogue on Orianenburg Strasse was set alight by the SA, but the chief of police, to his credit, aware of the building's historical significance, called the fire brigade and much of the synagogue was saved.

All around the Jewish area of Berlin where Miriam and Joe lived, gangs of youths roamed, breaking windows of Jewish properties, ransacking and looting as they went. The windows of Miriam's knitwear shop on Grosse Frankfurter Strasse were shattered, the place ransacked and the furniture was thrown into the street to be burned. The merchandise was looted by neighbours and customers whom they had considered to be their friends. It was a lonely time for Miriam as she no longer could lean on the support of her beloved husband, Jacub. Luckily the flat on Friedenstrasse in a tenement building was not damaged.

This terrible event became known as Kristallnacht (the Night of the Broken Glass) because of the shards of glass splintered all over the pavements and streets. It was quite clear that the violence was not spontaneous. It had been comprehensively organised by the Nazi authorities. Miriam, like thousands of others, was forced to clear up all the debris left by Nazi thugs in the certain knowledge that her livelihood had come to an abrupt end. How would she look after her son? Within herself she decided that Joe should continue to go to school, and that now he was old enough, he should prepare for his Bar Mitzvah. This would help to keep him focused and hopefully unaware of the very practical problems she was facing.

Knowing that Polish Jewish wives would be desperate to follow their husbands, the Nazis forced them to pay for the damage perpetrated by SA thugs and civilians before leaving the country. Since the insurance money had been confiscated by the authorities, and Miriam had insufficient funds to meet the cost of repairs, Jacub's family in Lodz had no option but to send her the money. When she needed money for food, she would have to seek help from the Jewish emergency services.

Quite apart from the death and destruction during those two days, Kristallnacht had a devastating psychological effect on the Jews of Germany and Austria. It presaged what was to come. The Nazis meant business, and from that date, any Jews who had soldiered on amid all the developing persecution over the previous five years, imagining and hoping that things would improve, on that November night knew that the opposite was true. No Jew felt safe in Germany anymore, as every day was lived in constant fear of arrest and imprisonment. The desire to leave the country became frantic.

Adolf Eichmann was given the task of accelerating Jewish emigration in January 1939 at the Zentralstelle für Judische Auswanderung... the Central Office for Jewish Emigration. He located all the relevant agencies into one place, and then allowed the Zionist organisations to operate them. Money extracted from prosperous Jews was used to fund the emigration of the poor. He organised an 'assembly line' system whereby a Jew could reach the office and proceed from desk to desk until he arrived finally with a passport and an exit visa, but stripped of his property, cash and rights. Within a few months the office had authorised the emigration of a hundred and fifty thousand Jews, and considerably lined the Nazi coffers.

War was brewing, and Germany was preparing to

expand further her territorial claims in Europe. In England, following the terror of Kristallnacht, an emergency government cabinet meeting was held regarding the plight of the Jews in Germany, and it was decided that the country should accept ten thousand mainly Jewish children from Germany, Austria, Czechoslovakia and Poland but without their parents. Very widespread public concern in the UK, within the Jewish and non-Jewish communities, generated the necessary finance, organisation and hospitality. An organisation which became known as the Kindertransport was operated by both Jewish and non-Jewish agencies, including the Quakers. The first transportation took place remarkably quickly, on 1st December 1938, and involved two hundred children living in orphanages which had been destroyed by the Kristallnacht pogrom and whose parents had been arrested by the Nazis. These children were considered to be at greatest risk.

Miriam realised the extreme danger to her son if he stayed in Germany or even Poland, and she also knew that Jacub's cousin, Leah, was married to an Englishman and living in St John's Wood, London. Would Joe be able to stay with them? She made her way to the Central Office of Jewish Emigration to find out the necessary details, and then she contacted Leah and Mark begging them to invite Joe to Britain, to provide him with a home and to sponsor him with a guarantee of fifty pounds so that he would not become a burden on the British government. Fortunately, Leah and Mark had the funds to promise this, and needed no further persuasion.

In the months following, Joe continued with his

studies, and since all Jewish children were expelled from state schools in 1938, the school at Grosse Hamburger Strasse became even more crowded. For all that Joe was able to make his Bar Mitzvah with a group of boys, including Sam Blomberg, in the spring of 1939, but he was very sad that his father could not be present at such an important time. David Blomberg, like Jacub, had been expelled back to Poland, leaving the four children with Rosa, so the fatherless situation applied to Sam too.

At the end of May 1939, Miriam accompanied Joe to Friedrichstrasse railway station, and there he boarded a train with three hundred other German Jewish children destined for the Hook of Holland. He, like the other youngsters, carried only one small labelled suitcase, a satchel with food and a few possessions in it, no valuables and no more than ten marks in cash. Each child travelled with a numbered tag on the front of their clothing, and another tag with their name on the back. Joe's passport had a large red J for Jew stamped on it, and, following Nazi orders, his tag bore the extra name 'Israel' to show that he was a Jew.

On that platform the emotion was palpable… small children heartbroken to leave their parents, older ones protective of their siblings, mothers wiping tears from their eyes, teenage boys anticipating an adventure, young adolescent girls proud of wearing their very best clothes, grandfathers looking depressed and weary, but making the best of a sad situation, and very tiny children who were too young to travel, destined to a terrible fate. Many of the fathers were missing having been expelled back to Poland like Jacub and David, or were imprisoned in Buchenwald, Sachsenhausen or Dachau.

Miriam and Joe hugged and kissed each other before he boarded the train. With tears in her eyes, Miriam told him that she was proud of him, that as he was going to safety in England, he should do his very best there and cooperate with Leah and Mark. She wanted to know how he would settle into his new life, so please write, and she assured him that she and his father would be in contact as soon as possible. She turned and waved at him as she watched the train chug its way out of the station. She felt very alone.

Returning to the flat on Friedenstrasse, Miriam cried wretchedly, and recalled the time when she had given birth to Joe; that overwhelming bond, that feeling of love and protection. She wanted to feel courageous for having sent her only child to England, to an alien environment, but all she could feel was anger and bitterness for being separated from those she loved most. She was desperate to leave Berlin now, to join Jacub in Lodz, but after settling bills, there was no money to pay the emigration tax. Again, the family in Lodz was able to produce the amount she needed, and finally she was free to leave.

Chapter 7
England

Joe's mind was swimming with thoughts as he sat silently in the railway carriage staring ahead of himself. He recognised a few faces from the Judische Freyschule, but none of them were his friends. He wondered about Sam Blomberg. Why wasn't he on the train? They could have travelled together and felt much better in each other's company. Was he to travel on the next transport? As it was, his mother had hinted that Sam would be staying in Berlin for the time being, so he must be going to Lodz with his mother and family to join his father, David Blomberg. Why couldn't he do the same thing, and be with *his* parents? They could have stayed in Lodz all together. It just wasn't fair. Although she was his father's cousin, he had never met this Leah, who had been married to a Londoner for a number of years.

Children of all ages were on the train, and some were already consuming the food in their satchels. Others, little ones, were crying for their mothers, and not wanting to eat at all. The journey through Germany seemed to take forever, and the Gestapo officer whose job it was to keep them all in order made the time pass even more slowly. After some hours the children had eaten all the sandwiches and apples their parents had packed for them. They felt tired, hungry, dirty, bored and uncomfortable on the hard, wooden benches. At the German side of the Dutch border, more members of the railway police joined the train to check that the children would take nothing valuable out of the country. Then when the Gestapo agent and all the officers got out and the train moved into Holland, a cheer went up, at first from a few older boys and then others joined them. They had escaped from Nazi Germany!

The train slowed down to a stop on the Dutch side, and in came some volunteers, smiling ladies bringing jugs of hot chocolate, dumplings, sandwiches and biscuits with them. They welcomed the youngsters with open arms and made them feel that somebody cared about them... that not everyone in this world behaved like Nazis. Their kindness and nurturing were exactly what the children needed, and enabled the youngest ones to sleep until they reached the coast. Aboard, there was also an adult member of the German Jewish community who was able to help very young, tearful travellers, and to answer the children's questions. The train journey came to an end at the Hook of Holland, and from there the three hundred refugee children trudged their way to the ferry bound for Harwich.

The crossing took about eight hours, and although it was the month of May, a powerful wind was blowing from the west, bringing rain with it and making a turbulent English Channel and North Sea. Many of the children were seasick and distressed and sleepless. Two English Quaker volunteers crossed with them and ministered to their needs, particularly the little ones. By early morning the wind had dropped, and the rain had ceased as the ferry approached Harwich in north-east Essex. The children were exhausted and disoriented when the boat docked at Parkeston Quay.

Joe was glad and relieved to get off the ferry. In spite of staggering to a bunk bed in a cabin shared with three other boys, he had been very seasick during the night and felt thoroughly wretched, wishing he was back home in his own bed. He had not wanted to eat anything for hours, but now he felt ravenous. Everything seemed so strange. All the signs, names and instructions were in English and he could not understand a word.

After taking breakfast on the ferry, the children were divided into two main groups by British organisers from the Refugee Children's Movement. Those without prearranged foster families were to be sheltered at temporary centres in holiday camps such as Dovercourt, which was not far from Harwich, whereas those to be met by their foster families would take the train to Liverpool Street in London.

Joe wondered how long this journey would take and looking at a nearby map he deduced that the train would have to cross the county of Essex to reach London. Fortified by a hot breakfast, he boarded the train, found himself a window seat and began to take an interest in what he observed. After leaving the docks of a busy international sea port, they steamed through rolling countryside, passing villages and hamlets, wheat fields and windmills, thatched cottages and farmhouses. Joe noticed the towns of Colchester and Chelmsford, but as the train approached East London, slums, docks, factories, smoke, grime and poverty had replaced the picturesque countryside of North Essex. The journey took about two hours which was a lot shorter than travelling through Germany and Holland, Joe noted. He began to feel nervous about meeting his relative, Leah, at Liverpool Street Station. He didn't know why exactly, but everything was so strange and unnerving. As the train slowed down to its terminus, he put his head out of the window and noticed a crowd of waiting people, some with placards with names written on them, smiling and waving. His name and number were checked by an organiser who led him to a couple waiting near the barrier, Leah and Mark Lewandowski.

Leah hugged him warmly, and wished him, "Welcome to England" in Yiddish! It was such a blessing for Joe to hear the familiar language of Ashkenazi Jews and to feel welcomed and accepted. Mark shook both his hands warmly, and then taking hold of Joe's case, he directed them all to a waiting car near the station, driven by a family friend. As they drove to St John's Wood, Joe said very little, relieved to have arrived safely, but very, very tired. His eyes felt heavy as the engine purred along, and he dozed off amid the to and fro of Yiddish conversation. He even missed seeing the famous red London double decker buses.

On reaching the Lewandowskis' home in St John's Wood, Joe was shown to his room on the ground floor situated next to the music room. He was already aware that Mark was a professional musician... in fact a concert singer, a composer, voice teacher and conductor... but he had a very easy, friendly way with him. People like Mark had never crossed his path before; musical Jews in Berlin were banned from their careers, and like all other Jews in that city, they were forever anxious and stressed about what the future would bring. It was different here. After a bath and a hot meal, he thanked his new family, unpacked his case, placed the photo of his parents by his bedside and then fell fast asleep for many hours.

The next day, Mark and Leah's two children arrived, having spent a few days with their aunt in Kent, and Joe was invited to explore the house with them. In common with most of the properties in the terrace, it had been built during the Regency period and provided plenty of space. A basement housed the kitchen, scullery, dining room, larder, lavatory and a coal cellar. The sitting room on the ground floor which had now become Joe's room had served as a waiting room for pupils. Another lavatory was situated on the staircase leading up to three bedrooms and a bathroom. On the floor above, an attic contained water tanks, trunks and storage. The garden was mostly given to lawn and fruit trees.

The two children, Robert and Janet, were aged ten years and six years respectively, and unlike their parents spoke only English. Robert, a studious boy, attended a prep school in St John's Wood, was learning to play the violin and was very musical like his father. Jane, confident and lively, was at a local state primary school for the time being. Their parents were agnostic secular Jews and did not encourage Roger and Jane to attend a synagogue or learn Hebrew. At table a great deal of translation went on, mainly from Leah, so that Joe would be included in the conversation. The children taught him a few necessary words when they were playing ball in the garden, and he clearly enjoyed the family atmosphere which as an only child was new to him. Aware of the horrors perpetrated against the Jews in Germany, Mark and Leah were delighted to see Joe smile and enjoy himself.

Life in the music room was sacrosanct and busy. Mark was either practising or rehearsing for concerts all over Britain, or teaching his many pupils, but during August the whole family would spend a month in the Essex countryside near Saffron Walden with other music-loving friends. Of course, this year Joe accompanied them; in fact when war broke out on 3rd September, they were all extending the holiday, and the three children were wearing their gas masks whilst picking blackberries in the fields near the house. Mark and Leah decided to keep the family out of London temporarily, away from any hostilities, until they had considered a plan of action for the children. It was the time of the phoney war, and the bombs did not drop.

The outbreak of war accelerated the need for a decision about the children's education. As Jane was very young, she continued to attend the local school, and Roger was granted a music scholarship to a boarding school in Hampshire. Through contacting the Refugee Children's Movement again, Leah researched the educational possibilities for Joe, and was introduced to a Christian couple, Ian and Eileen Grundy, who were managing a small private school in Acton. They had decided that their contribution to the war effort would be to help two

Kindertransport children. Joe was one of them, and the second was Rolf Steinberg, a boy of similar age, who had arrived in England from Vienna on one of the last trains. The Grundy couple educated them without charge, giving them free board and lodging in their house during term-time. In the holidays they returned to their sponsors and Joe would be reunited with the Lewandowski family.

At first Joe had been cushioned into life in England by staying with relatives in a home where Polish, German and Yiddish as well as English were spoken, reminding him of home. Now he was immersed in an alien environment, no matter how well-meaning it was, where only English was spoken. In his letters to Jacub and Miriam he wrote about his terrible homesickness for them, especially at night, but also for Leah and Mark. During the first months of the war, letters were exchanged without a problem, fortunately. Jacub, who was always scholarly, wrote that he had taken to reciting English poetry at his home in Lodz, and looked forward to the time after the war when he and Miriam would join Joe in England. Jacub also mentioned that Rosa had joined her husband in Lodz and had brought her youngest children with her. With no relatives or contacts in England, Sam had begged his mother not to send him on the Kindertransport, and she had finally relented. Feeling so homesick at the time, Joe felt a tinge of envy shoot through him on reading this news. Why couldn't he be with them all in Lodz?

Eileen Grundy was fortunately a warm, understanding soul, well aware of the traumatic effects that leaving family and country would have on young children. She advised Joe to write regularly to his parents and to Leah and Mark in London, and to make them all proud by working hard at his studies, adding that he and Rolf would make more friends and generally feel better as soon as they could speak English. She then provided him with a basic English course which she and her husband had devised together.

Chapter 8
Litzmannstadt

By 1939 Lodz maintained a population of six hundred and sixty-five thousand, thirty-four per cent of whom were Jewish, ten per cent were German and the remainder mostly Polish. Soon after Joe's departure to England, Miriam left Berlin to join Jacub and family in Lodz, having paid for repairs and emigration tax, and taking with her one small suitcase of personal belongings, as allowed by the German authorities. During the journey, German Customs Officers searched her case many times, and like all Jews escaping Germany, she was forced to leave behind anything of value… jewellery, furniture or art… becoming a penniless beggar overnight, just like her husband, who had had no choice but to take only his hat, coat and passport.

Miriam's joyful relief to be reunited with Jacub and family as well as with her own relatives was overwhelming and helped to soften the pain she felt from Joe's absence. She and Jacub wrote to him often, giving him news of their lives in Lodz, and endeavouring to keep the letters as positive as possible. They set about finding employment and decided to rent a one-room apartment in Radogoszcz on the outskirts of the city in a German area, that of the Volksdeutsche or ethnic Germans living in Poland. Sadly,

Miriam's family in Lodz decided together, that life would be better for them in Warsaw. They packed and left to join other branches of their family in that city just before the outbreak of war.

On 1st September 1939, the Germans invaded Poland, annexing it to the Reich, and starting World War II. Although both Poles and Jews had fought hard to dig fortifications around the city, by 8th September the German army had occupied Lodz, renaming it Litzmannstadt after a general in World War I. Within days of their arrival, Jacub and Miriam felt very unwelcome by the German community in which they lived, and moved back to the family apartment in Zgierska Street. They took over the small room they used to occupy in their early married life, and unpacked their solitary suitcase.

One of the first orders in December 1939 sent from Berlin to Dr. Ubelhor, the president of Litzmannstadt, was to organise a ghetto, and these orders were published in newspapers and displayed on posters throughout the city. The Jewish Council, or Judenrat, was informed by the Gestapo that five hundred families would be removed from their homes into the ghetto each day. Forced out of their dwellings, intimidated and frightened, many had to find accommodation where they could. The Mendelson apartment, like many others, became open house to these poor evicted people, carrying just the bare essentials on their shoulders in freezing weather with several inches of snow underfoot and a yellow star sewn on the front and back of their clothing. Any form of non-cooperation with the Nazis or refusal to move resulted in extreme violence;

doors were smashed in and the inhabitants were shot. Then, in the middle of the night, the first deportations took place with fourteen thousand Jews taken from streets close to the Mendelson family to trains, never to return. After that, the housing situation became less severe.

The Nazis confiscated everything of value from the houses of those they were evicting... furniture, paintings, jewellery, furs, clothing, foreign currency... and was sold at ridiculously low prices to Germans in a currency used only in the ghetto and which had no value outside. In Plac Koscielny a church dedicated to the Assumption of the Blessed Virgin Mary was turned into a storehouse for stolen Jewish property. When the Mendelsons' turn came to give up their valuables, Jacub did not relinquish his gold watch quickly enough for the German police and he was badly beaten for it. Miriam dissolved into tears, unable to comprehend such unnecessary violence, and rushed to comfort her husband.

The ghetto was set up in the working-class neighbourhoods of the Old City, where the Germans built a special railway line to supply it with raw materials for the textile factories. That line was later used for deportations. The Mendelsons did not have to move as their apartment was located in a block already inside the ghetto, but by spring of 1940, about a hundred and sixty-three thousand people were crammed into a space of four-square kilometres, sealed off with walls and barbed wire, and guarded by six hundred German policemen. These were known as the Schutzpolizei. To qualify as members, they needed to have had previous military service, to be of

Aryan descent and to be members of the SS. Jewish police units were also established in the ghetto under Nazi occupation. Their job was to maintain public order, to fight epidemics and fires, to guard the ghetto walls and to enforce German orders. This included rounding up thousands of fellow Jews for deportation.

During the winter of 1939/40, with such overcrowding in a small area, little food and no proper medication, five thousand people died of malnutrition, dysentery, typhus and tuberculosis. The ghetto was sealed off so effectively and guarded so stringently that it was impossible to leave, to have knowledge of what went on in the Gentile part of the city or to be able to bargain for food from there. Since there was no sewerage system, as there was in Warsaw, it was impossible to escape via the sewers.

The Nazis appointed an elderly man named Mordechai Chaim Rumkowski as chairman of the Jewish Council, or Judenrat, to organise their various diktats. He believed that if the ghetto dwellers were transformed into an extremely useful workforce, then the Jews would be needed by the Nazis, and their usefulness would ensure that the ghetto would be supplied with food. He duly delivered a petition on these lines to the authorities, and it was agreed that the workers would be paid in food, only in food, and the amount was not mentioned. It turned out to be totally insufficient. To supplement a meagre diet, Rumkowski allocated small plots of land to various youth groups to grow vegetables. In the factories, adults and able youngsters were employed to produce many items... from textiles to munitions. Despite their experience in the rag trade, Jacub and Miriam opted to work at the ghetto post office, and that fact became an innocuous piece of news for Joe in one of their regular letters to him. They both missed him terribly but knew their decision to send him to England had been the right one. This was confirmed when they learned that young Sam Blomberg was working for bread in one of the textile factories.

Shimon, Jacub's younger brother, was thwarted in his desire to lead a religious life of study when the Nazis blew up all the synagogues and yeshivas of Lodz, deporting large numbers of ultra-Orthodox males to work on building autobahns. The Mendelson family never saw him again which broke his parents' hearts and that of Grandmother whose favourite he was. The apartment felt empty without him, and, with tears in their eyes, they hopelessly prayed for his return every Shabbat, yet knowing that many had already been deported and had never returned, recalling how the SS had humiliated so many Hasidim, pulling their earlocks and beards before beating them up. Grandmother wrung her hands and cried out pitifully that the world had gone stark raving mad. Life in the ghetto was the only life they knew now.

Somehow word was received through the use of banned radios that after the fall of so many countries... Norway, Denmark, Belgium, Holland and France... that the Battle of Britain was followed by the indiscriminate bombing of British cities and towns, most of all, London. Miriam was terrified since she knew that Joe was at school in Acton during term-time and in St John's Wood during the holidays. Both were in London, and to her it seemed that Joe must be in terrible danger. Perhaps it would have been better to have allowed him to stay with them in Lodz, as her friend Rosa told her when they met near the Baluty market one day in the winter of 1940/41, queueing up for food. Bombs were falling on London every night, with no let up, she said. Thousands of people had died and a million homes ruined. In reality, East London with its industry and docks, was being hit the hardest, but to those without knowledge of the city, it was difficult to understand.

In a panic, Miriam wrote immediately to the Lewandowskis and anxiously awaited their reply which finally reassured both her and Jacub. The Blitz, as the bombing was called, was badly affecting London and its suburbs, but the schools had been evacuated, some to Wales, Dorset, Devon and Cornwall, and Joe's school had been relocated to Henley-on-Thames in Oxfordshire. Leah added that Joe had settled and was well. In due course, Joe also wrote his own news to them, and that comforting letter was the last they were to receive before postal communication was cut off completely.

The queues for food were endless. Hours, and whole nights, were spent waiting for meagre rations, with sometimes no result except permanent hunger pains. Starvation in the winter was worst of all for elderly people who, from weakness, slipped and fell in the snow and mud, some never to get up again. It was a common occurrence to see poor souls face down, immobile in the snow. As time passed, nobody seemed to care about others, and as the months and years passed the rations shrank. The German

Jews who were more educated and used to a more prosperous life than the Polish Jews were the first to succumb to diseases, and many committed suicide. The living would often hide the deaths of their relatives for as long as possible in order to continue claiming their rations.

During the freezing winter the pipes burst in a city with no sewerage system. Toilets would not flush and human faecal waste was thrown out of some windows, along with other waste, onto the streets below, producing a horrendous stench. The toilets next to the tenements were always overflowing, and those who, according to the Nazis, had committed crimes were ordered to clean them up, and could be seen tainted with faeces. Disease spread, and thousands died from cold, starvation and filth. Miriam and Sara did what they could to keep the apartment clean by boiling water, but soap was always scarce. Jacub was the first in the morning to bring up water from the standpipe. Every day he would shave carefully and recite English poetry, before going to the ghetto post office where at lunch time he and Miriam would receive a bowl of thin soup in payment for their work. Like their friends and relatives, they were always hungry. Ezra helped to make German uniforms at one of the textile factories which had been originally owned by Jews, and Sara worked at one of the ghetto soup kitchens. Grandmother stayed at home, sometimes to nurse a sick person or to look after a baby whose mother was working. It became so cold in the winter months that they were forced to burn furniture to keep warm. Sheds, fences and outhouses were pulled down to provide extra fuel.

Sara's regular visits to the orphanage to occupy the children were terminated in September 1942 when Chaim Rumkovski agreed to honour the Nazi demands for children under ten years of age and adults over sixty-five years to be available for 're-settlement'. Too young or too old to be productive, they were considered to be a drain on the Reich, and were therefore ordered into wagons to be sent to a place called Chelmno, some eight-three kilometres to the north-west of the city and easily accessible by both rail and road. The victims were then directed into 'Spezialwagen', or gas vans, which looked rather like ambulances. When the motors were turned on, the carbon monoxide fumes were directed into the back of the vans, asphyxiating the trapped victims as they were driven to the Rzuchowski Forest where they were buried.

Sara's visits to the hospital followed the same pattern as the orphanage. The patients she used to know had all disappeared, as had the elderly at the old age home. Orphans who had escaped and lived on the streets had little chance of survival. With no ration book and no place to stay, it was just a matter of time. Their emaciated bodies could be found stiff on the pavements in the early morning.

Hans Biebow, the chief Nazi administrator of the Lodz ghetto, together with the help of Chaim Rumkowski, had managed to rid the area of unproductive people. Over seventy thousand Jews and five thousand gypsies had been gassed at Chelmno, and now the ghetto resembled a forced labour camp. Everyone was working hard producing huge amounts of goods for the Reich in exchange for bread and a daily bowl of soup. For that reason, deportations, on a grand scale, ceased between September 1942 and May 1944, excluding about fifty thousand Jews from outside Lodz who were brought in and then summarily dispatched to Chelmno.

That Grandmother managed to survive the earlier deportations was due to sheer luck and the fact that she never went out, but this luck came to an end in the winter of 1942/43. It so happened that while the rest of the family were working, she was sharing her ration with a young twelve-year-old orphan, hiding him in a room nearby which had once belonged to her old friend, Esther, who had died recently from typhus. Grandmother fell ill from lack of food, developed pneumonia and died quickly. She was seventy-nine years old.

The young orphan, Dov Friedman, whom the Mendelsons took on was truly sad at the death of his benefactor, as of course was the family who had no idea that Grandmother had kept him in hiding. The young boy was also terrified that now he would be handed over to the authorities. He had reminded her of Shimon, her grandson, who had been rounded up by the Nazis to help build an autobahn and had never returned. Grandmother was buried as soon as possible in the Jewish cemetery near Radogoszcz station. It was from this station that so many thousands were sent to their deaths.

The main problem with Dov was that he had no ration card, and therefore the family would be expected to share their meagre amounts of food with him. They all knew that Grandmother would want them to do just that. Otherwise he would become yet another death statistic, frozen solid on a wintry pavement. Before the war Ezra had been well-placed in the fruit and vegetable business, so his contacts would be able to tell him where to find a few extra potatoes from time to time, and a talented artist friend would be able to design a false ration card in secret. It was risky, and it would cost a fair bit, but for Grandmother's memory he would do it. And so Dov became a member of the Mendelson household, and they found him to be very savvy for his age about life in the ghetto. He knew the best times to go out to avoid the Gestapo or the Jewish police, he could outrun all of them and hide in the unlikeliest of places until the danger had passed. His small, wiry frame was definitely an asset.

Rumkowski delivered notice that a five p.m. curfew would be introduced into the ghetto operating from 5th September 1942, and that anyone found in the street without a movement permit would be deported. Dov was the only one in the Mendelson household to disregard this new law despite warnings from Jacub and Miriam. Both his parents were dead, and he was a law unto himself.

Chapter 9
The Ghetto Years Roll On

In 1943, after the Warsaw uprising which the Lodz inhabitants heard about on their clandestine radios, the deportations continued to a lesser extent. Hans Biebow visited the ghetto factories to inform the workers that greater productivity was expected, but that due to wartime shortages there would be less food. Thus, the ghetto supply of rations dwindled further to a bare minimum, causing sickness and the death rate to rise, and productivity to fall. It was well-known that many slept with their bread ration under their pillows to avoid theft.

Ezra became thinner and thinner, his face puffed up and his legs were distended. When he caught Dov unloading some potatoes and carrots hidden in his trousers, he was angry at the theft, even though everyone was starving, and told him never to do it again. Sara was more lenient, understanding his adolescent hunger, but for days she had been unable to work, running a temperature with nausea and vomiting, a headache and cough. Then a red rash started to spread over her body, and she appeared not to know what was going on around her. Jacub and Miriam were intensely worried about her, so Jacub hurried to search for Berish Kaplinsky, a doctor friend he knew in the ghetto, and begged him to visit Sara. Berish took very little time to diagnose typhus which he said was a bacterial infection caused by the common louse. His face was very grave as he explained that he had virtually no access to medicines, but he did have some disinfectant. He told Miriam to scrub the floors with it to prevent further infection, and to sponge Sara down to lower the fever. He also left a few aspirin, and said he could by no means guarantee that she would survive. That was in the hands of God.

Sara's recovery took many weeks, and was not aided by the poor nutrition forced on all members of the ghetto. She never regained her former strength. Dov managed to produce soap from somewhere which helped to keep the place clean, and at night he would defy the curfew to purloin more vegetables for their soup, making certain they were kept out of Ezra's sight. It was so cold that the whole family went to bed wearing their outdoor clothes, including woolly hats.

One afternoon in February 1943, Miriam happened to meet David Blomberg outside the post office, and was aghast at his haggard appearance. Neither she nor Jacub had seen him since Grandmother had died, and even then, it was a fleeting wave on the way to work; they weren't even sure where he and Rosa lived anymore, and now that the curfew was in operation, visits were even less likely. Miriam realised that David had made a special effort to see her, and he had difficulty speaking, tears pouring down his face and beard. Eventually he choked out news that their youngest child had been very sick, that Rosa had refused to be separated from her, and had lost her mind from the agony of it all. Both had gone to be 'resettled', which he knew meant no return. Only he and Sam remained. By this time, Jacub had arrived on the scene, and they suggested taking David home, but he would not hear of it and shuffled off, muttering that he needed to find Sam.

Such a change in a man was stupefying. In Berlin he had been full of life, confidence and humour, despite all their difficulties, and on Shabbat, as one of the cantors at the Oranienburger Synagogue, his rich, deep, velvety bass voice would ring out in that large building, bringing comfort and joy to the congregation. Now he was a shell of a man, and Jacub wondered what he could do to help him. David needed to express his grief in music, but the Nazis had banned Jewish services of any sort, insisting that factory production continued on the Sabbath. In September 1942 many rabbis were murdered in Chelmno, others were absorbed into the administration, and marriages were performed by Rumkowski himself.

As usual, Dov was a source of information. He knew of certain cellars where rabbis conducted services, and where youngsters were posted outside to watch for the German police and warn the worshippers. It was unwise to use the same location twice running or to attend in large numbers. David received word of where a service would be held, and was able to sing Kaddish for his wife and child, as well as for all those who had died in the ghetto or who had been deported. Sam was also present, and it was clear to all that he had inherited his father's musical ability.

News soon spread that four men who had just arrived in the ghetto had worked on the Reichsautobahn, connecting Berlin to Posen. Jacub was keen to know about Shimon, his brother, who, with a number of other young men, had been forced to work on that autobahn, and he wanted to be able to give a message of hope to Sara and Ezra. With grim expressions, the men explained that a German engineer had assured them that the Spezialwagen had been in use for over two years there, and that those unable to continue working were sent to these ambulance-like vehicles with red crosses painted on them, and gassed with carbon monoxide. They had not heard of Shimon Mendelson. Jacub felt sick with fear, knowing that his brother had a weak constitution and little stamina for such gruelling work. Most of all he realised that all Jews were doomed. He had to keep this terrible secret to himself, and not tell Ezra and Sara... not even Miriam; it weighed on his mind, day and night, as he tried to feign normality.

In December 1943, whilst Nazi leaders of the Final Solution Committee were in conference, the struggle for survival in the Lodz ghetto continued amid snow blizzards and violent, biting winds. Inside the tenements frost formed inches deep on the walls, and outside listless, frozen people moved lethargically to await their rations in the icy streets. The cold was not all they feared. On orders from the Nazis they could be captured by the Jewish police and handed over to the Germans for deportation, so they constantly looked over their shoulders to avoid being caught. Bread was the most important part of the ghetto diet, and those who were unable to control their hunger consumed in one meal a loaf which was expected to last eight days. Sara was in charge of the food in the

Mendelson household, and always made it last until the next ration.

Despite all the misery of the Lodz ghetto, Jewish culture was kept alive since the inhabitants hungered for freedom of expression as well as for bread. Many plays and concerts were produced in the House of Culture (which seated four hundred), and occasionally religious services, held secretly from the Nazis. Schools and classes were organised in apartments and cellars, with poetry and reading groups. Dov, along with other students, hid his books under his clothing. Street singers sang songs of how life was in the ghetto, and there was even a Lodz Choral Society. Jacub and Miriam attended Zionist meetings, as they had done in Berlin, in the hope that after the war they could emigrate to Palestine with their son Joe. These activities ceased to exist by around 1942, and certainly by 1943, due to deportations, starvation and disease. Thousands died in the ghetto without the need to deport them.

Even though the rations were reduced again in 1944, the Lodz Jews had reason to be optimistic. Those who had access to radios and newspapers reported that the Russians had trounced the Germans in Belarus and were now approaching Warsaw. The allies were progressing up Italy to the south of France, and a mass invasion of northern France was imminent. Jacub and Miriam had reason to think that the war would be over soon, and they would be reunited with Joe. Their dream of seeing him was always uppermost in their minds, and within the ghetto it was a question of hanging on and sticking it out. In May the spring sun thawed the frozen toilets and produced an unbearable stench.

By this time, all other ghettos in Poland had been liquidated, and yet seventy-seven thousand Jews remained in Lodz due its industrial output. Hans Biebow and Artur Greiser, the Nazi chief of the Warthegau, were both keen for the production to continue as it not only filled the coffers of the Third Reich, but made them millionaires as well. Heinrich Himmler thought differently. Knowing that the Germans were losing the war, he was insistent that the Final Solution should continue as soon as possible. Thus, in June 1944 he ordered the liquidation of the Lodz ghetto, and for deportations to Chelmno to start again. Within a few weeks over seven thousand Jews perished there. These round-ups continued throughout July.

Himmler realised that the Russians were rapidly approaching in the East, and that as the Chelmno gas vans were proving too slow and inefficient to achieve the Final Solution, to liquidate the Lodz ghetto would mean the remaining thousands should be sent to Auschwitz where their demise would be quicker. Lists were compiled of those to be 'resettled', with promises not to separate families. Work and food would be provided in comfortable surroundings. Several hundred reported to the Radogosczc railway station, but the vast majority did not, preferring to hide from the Gestapo, the German police and the Jewish Sonderkommando. Placards from Rumkowski appeared on the ghetto walls, but nobody bothered to read them. The Sonderkommando and police could not fill the cattle trains, so every time the population resisted evacuation, the food rations were cut. One family, neighbours of the Mendelsons, had one by one died of starvation, like hundreds of others. Their other neighbours had already been deported.

Dov always seemed to know where to find extra food, and what was going on. On 9th August he reported that the Einsatzgruppen who had returned from a killing spree of tens of thousands of Jews in Belarus and the Ukraine had marched into Lodz following the orders of Heinrich Himmler, and were surrounding every block in turn. They searched every room, cellar and attic. Walls were tapped and tested. Dov also reported that David and Sam Blomberg had been rounded up from their apartment. That news depressed and saddened Jacub and Miriam, and silently they were again grateful that Joe was relatively safe in England.

In spite of this information, Miriam, Jacub, Ezra and Sara were united in their decision to resist deportation. With great difficulty and little energy, Ezra and Jacub pushed heavy double beds against the closed door, and they all found a hiding place in an enormous wardrobe with a false back. There they hoped to stay until the Germans had gone, and, who knows, until they were liberated by the Russians. They would hang on. Jacub and Miriam thought more than ever of a reunion with Joe in England. When the police and Jewish Sonderkommando had gone temporarily, they would emerge from their cramped hiding place to stretch their legs. Their stock of food was reducing, but they dared not go out into the deserted streets. In the distance they could hear artillery fire from the Russians in the east, around Warsaw, and air raids. It would surely not be long before their liberation.

One warm, sunny morning at the end of August, Dov ventured out early to try to locate food for the family since they could no longer use their ration cards. He cautiously opened the gate leading onto the street, imagining that owing to the round-ups the streets would be empty, when to his horror he saw a group of Einsatzcommandos on the other side of the street, casually smoking in the sunshine. Panic-stricken, he gasped, and as he did so, they spotted him. He raced off, pursued by one rather corpulent commando into a labyrinth of passages, empty apartments and yards. Shots rang out, but none hit the target, and Dov, whose knowledge of the area was second to none, was able to outrun the German until he took refuge in one of his many hiding places. From there he heard, "*Du schmutziger Jude*" (you dirty Jew), many times, before the soldier gave up the chase.

Incensed that they had failed to capture Dov, the Einsatzcommandos stormed back to the Mendelsons' tenement on Zgierska Street and surrounded it, screaming vile, antisemitic insults and crashing on the doors. The whole empty building reverberated with the sound of bullets as they threatened to shoot their way into the apartment. Ezra called out that shooting would be unnecessary as they would unblock the door. He and Jacub moved the beds away from the entrance; Sara, overwrought, burst into uncontrollable tears and Miriam was weeping quietly. Their plans had failed, and they knew what their future would be. Ezra's head drooped as if to express that he had given up. He opened the door, his arm around Sara who was sobbing and trembling with fear. They stumbled out to an open cart, in the heat of the day, followed by Jacub and Miriam, pale and silent with shock from the trauma. They were transported to Radogoszcz railway station where they were to be loaded into cattle wagons en route for Auschwitz.

Hiding in an empty attic nearby, Dov Friedman saw his friends depart... but he never saw them again.

Chapter 10
Education

Letters from his parents no longer reached him and Joe was worried and sad. News from home always made him feel good, even though 'home' was now Lodz in Poland, and not in Berlin where he was born. Home was where his parents and grandparents were. And come to think of it, that included his friend, Sam Blomberg, who had gone to Lodz with his family and not joined the Kindertransport.

Joe's Aunt Leah in London had elderly parents, two sisters and numerous aunts, uncles and cousins in Poland, who had also stopped corresponding. Mr Grundy, who was head of the small prep school where Joe was studying, told him that the war was the cause of this non-communication, and that other countries were similarly affected, but Joe was silently unconvinced, since he knew that his mother and father actually worked in the Lodz Ghetto post office. Surely, they were in the best situation for sending letters. He was baffled. Fortunately, Leah and Mark Lewandowski wrote to him in term-time, giving him their news and that of the children, and Joe always looked forward to returning to St John's Wood in the holidays to be with his English family. Music reigned there, and plenty of fun with his cousins and a chance to speak German or Yiddish with Aunt Leah and Uncle Mark. That helped to soften the sense of inner loneliness he had carried around with him since he left Berlin.

The loneliness affected him most of all at night before he went to sleep, and thoughts of his parents crowded his mind. Why had he not accompanied his mother to Lodz like Sam Blomberg? He could have helped and protected her on the journey, but she was so firm about sending him to England. He sometimes wondered if his parents wanted rid of him, but then, recalling his mother's tearful face at the station, banished the thought from his mind until the next time. He remembered clearly the wretched time in Berlin; their shop being boycotted, and the need to be very careful with money; the jeering and disdain at the state school, the loss of non-Jewish friends and the bullying in the schoolyard after lessons. Even the Jewish school could not prevent bullying on the way home, and how many non-Jewish adults would defend a Jewish child? Fewer and fewer, he had discovered.

Sometimes thoughts of the Gestapo poisoned his mind as he recalled the terrifying scene in October 1938 when two agents took his father away one evening with just his hat, coat and passport, and expelled him back to Poland along with sixteen thousand other Polish nationals. Joe had been trembling with fear in his bed and, pretending to be asleep, he had been unable to say goodbye to Jacub. Now he felt so guilty and hoped his father would be able to forgive him. Then in November of the same year, when he and his mother were living alone in Berlin, the catastrophic events of Kristallnacht were just not something you read about in the papers. Upset by the violence perpetrated on the knitwear shop, Miriam had discovered that the whole place had been wrecked and the stock looted by people they considered their friends. Joe could not help his mother and felt guilty about it. She had insisted that he return to school in the morning while she had cleared up the shards of glass and ruined fitments only to be informed that she would have to pay for the repairs. The Gestapo were not interested in insurance... that would revert to the Reich... and his poor mother had just not had the money to afford the repair work. Yet she could not return to Poland without paying. Relatives in Lodz had had to send her the money. To add insult to injury, after she had paid for all the repairs, the Gestapo had made sure that a non-Jew took the shop out of her hands.

In the Jewish quarters of Berlin, Joe remembered the destruction everywhere, the shattering of glass and wrecking of property, the panic-stricken women whose husbands had been rounded up or shot, the children screaming and the smoke from the burning synagogues, the bullying on the streets and the shortage of money. His mother had been beside herself at times and always worried about what to do. The atmosphere in the city had been so violent that he had been scared to go to school, and when he did, many other pupils had stayed away. He had returned home by Jewish areas so that he could hide under market stalls if necessary, and avoid the stones thrown by non-Jewish hooligans.

During the day his mother had been in contact with those who might help... rabbis, friends, teachers, acquaintances... to find out how she could free Joe from this toxic and terrifying city. So many Jewish families had been intent on solving the same problem, and already thousands had fled abroad; some even as far as to Shanghai. But now Jacub had been expelled to Poland, and anyway as a couple, the cost of such a journey was beyond their means.

Fortunately, a rabbi who knew the Mendelsons at the New Synagogue in Scheuneunviertel before it had been set on fire had been able to tell Miriam about Kindertransport, the British initiative of inviting ten thousand Jewish children from Germany, Austria and Czechoslovakia into Britain following Kristallnacht. The procedure of obtaining a place on the Kindertransport, he had said, was to send an application form and a photograph to the local representative of the Refugee Children's Movement in Berlin. Then Miriam had contacted her cousin in London. Joe recalled the tears in her eyes when she had said goodbye at the station, reassuring him that the separation was only temporary and that he should do his very best. All these thoughts returned to mind at bedtime, and sometimes when Eileen Grundy came to say goodnight, he was crying quietly into his pillow. She took his hand, and assured him the homesickness would pass, and that working hard to do his very best would make his parents proud after the war when next he saw them.

During the weekdays, life was very active and challenging with all the subjects being taught in English rather than German. Ian Grundy arranged for special English lessons taught by a German speaker for both Joe and Rolf on a Wednesday afternoon when the rest of the boys were involved with sport. Both boys were intelligent, and they started to compete with one another in lesson time for the highest marks. Within a few months they could speak and understand well, and later, with encouragement to read as much as possible, the special lessons stopped. Sport was also encouraged in prep schools on Saturday afternoons, and in the summer Joe and Rolf were introduced to cricket, which was new and strange to them.

Rolf was nearly fifteen years old, the only son of elderly parents in Austria, and like Joe, he no longer received Red Cross letters or postcards from them. His last letter was returned which worried him, but he assumed it was due to the chaos of war. His older sister, Lotte, was studying music in America and she kept in touch regularly. Rolf had dreams of joining her after the war since he was gifted musically too and wished to become a concert pianist. Mr Grundy arranged for him to resume his music lessons and maintained the school grand piano to concert pitch.

Joe's gifts were intellectual, and once he had received a real grounding in English, he excelled in most subjects. One night before he went to sleep, he decided to study the English language seriously, if given the chance, keeping in his mind the words of his mother to do his very best and to make his parents proud. That would mean studying at university. With this in mind, he frequented the school library as often as time would allow, and invariably could be found there, absorbed in a book.

During the summer of 1940, the Battle of Britain was fought over the Channel and South of England, and bombs would then be dropped on London, mainly in the East End at first, from 7th September 1940, to smash the industry and docks. Ian and Eileen Grundy had realised that it was time to get out of Acton and to transfer the school to a safer area, namely to Ship Lake House in Henley-on-Thames. It was a more spacious building than the one at Cumberland Park, with the benefit of fields and, of course, the Thames. Acton was bombed numerous times from October until May 1941; in fact, in that time a member of a German bomber crew bailed out over Acton, and landed in a tree, much to the surprise of the residents. Henley-on-Thames and Oxfordshire in general were much safer places. Joe would spend little time there since that summer Ian Grundy realised that Joe had made outstanding progress in the previous year, and academically would benefit from the challenges of a senior school.

Joe returned to St John's Wood to spend all the holidays with the Lewandowskis and to share their family life. When not engaged in concerts and singing lessons, Mark was a member of the Auxiliary Fire Service and was ready to be called out at night to cope with fires caused by incendiary bombs. All three children were now attending boarding schools in the countryside for safety's sake. Leah, with her knowledge of Polish and German, was working in a secret, confidential job for the government and therefore remained in London for the duration of the war. She constantly worried about her family in Poland, but did not say too much in front of Joe. The whole family were amazed at Joe's language progress. He only needed to lapse into German or Yiddish when he met some of

Mark's musician friends who had escaped from Austria to Britain in the 1930s, and were attending Dame Myra Hess's concerts at the National Gallery. Later, he thought how lucky these adults were, although previously some had been forced to scrub the streets of Vienna. How he wished that his own parents had been able to obtain visas, and he felt guilty about his own good fortune.

On the pupils' return to school after the Easter holidays in 1940, Mr Grundy had the opportunity to prepare those who were leaving for their new schools. He explained to Joe that prep schools and private schools generally entered their pupils for the Common Entrance examination aged around thirteen plus to go to public school. In the case of gifted applicants, they could be accepted on scholarship: board, lodging and education being completely free of fees. Mr Grundy suggested that Joe might want to enter on scholarship at the age of fourteen. Keen to grasp this challenge and to be able to make his parents proud, Joe was delighted to knuckle down to study all the subjects on the curriculum, including Latin. Rolf was being prepared to take a scholarship to enter the Royal College of Music later on.

Joe passed the examinations into Hereford Cathedral School without difficulty as a scholar, though not as a chorister, and started there in September 1940. Again, it was another change of school, but he was now fourteen, had toughened up a little, and, to his great interest, he noted that other Jewish boys from abroad were studying there. This fact increased his confidence, and he grasped the academic challenge with resolve and a sense of competition. He also interested himself in some of the societies the school offered... chess, the debating society, table tennis and rowing on the River Wye. Other sports... rugby and cricket... were tolerated rather than enjoyed.

As far as Judaism was concerned, Ian Grundy had not made any definite arrangements for the boys to attend a synagogue, and when, months earlier, a rabbi had arrived to interview them, he had pointed out the location of the Ealing Synagogue which was not too far distant. Neither Joe nor Rolf had Orthodox backgrounds, and although both of them were proud to be Jews, and had made their Bar Mitzvah, they were not keen to attend shul weekly... perhaps at Pesach, Rosh Hashanah and Yom Kippur. Henley-on-Thames was lacking a synagogue and at Hereford it would have meant travelling to Worcester for the nearest one. Jewish boys at Hereford Cathedral School could choose whether or not to attend Christian services and were not forced to be present at religious education lessons. This 'free' time could be used advantageously for study, and occasionally a rabbi would visit and check on their spiritual welfare.

Together with other newcomers to Hereford, Joe was immediately plunged into studying for the School Certificate in numerous subjects which he took and passed at the end of the year at the age of fourteen. He flourished particularly in languages... Latin, Greek, German, English and French... and won a prize in Latin for having gained 90% in a competition subjects since many of the masters were now serving in the forces and not easily or effectively replaced.

Academic success developed Joe's confidence generally, but so did being speaker in the school's debating society in November 1941, when another Kindertransport pupil proposed that "America should make an official declaration of war on Germany." The two German Jewish boys who took part, must have had strong feelings about it, but the motion was lost by fourteen votes to sixteen. Within a very short time, however, on 7th December, the Japanese attacked Pearl Harbour which brought the USA into the war. Joe continued to be a member of the debating society during his years at Hereford, and later joined the Shakespearian society, not so much for the acting but to gain knowledge of the plays.

During the academic year 1941–42 Joe was a member of VI Classical, studying for the Higher Certificate which he passed when aged sixteen, and which would have enabled him to gain a place at university, but without a scholarship. The university authorities thought him too young for entry, so he stayed at Hereford for another year and gained a full classical scholarship to King's College Cambridge for September 1943 at age seventeen. He, the Lewandowskis and the Grundies were truly delighted, as were the headmaster and staff at Hereford Cathedral School. Joe had studied tremendously hard and thoroughly deserved their congratulations. It was sad that his parents could not be informed.

During the summer of 1942, the most blood-chilling news arrived from partisans in Poland concerning the horrendous treatment of Jews in eastern Europe. This was passed on to the BBC and appeared in the national newspapers. Joe read about it, though not in great detail, and worried about the situation of his parents, grandparents and other relatives in Lodz. On returning to St John's Wood in the summer holidays, he shared his worries with his Aunt Leah. They both felt equally guilty to be alive; he because Kindertransport had saved him from disaster, and she because she had left the family to marry an Englishman. Mark advised them not to think the worst. Worry would not help, and anyway might be needless. Easier said than done.

In his final term at Hereford, Joe enjoyed the honour of having gained the classical scholarship to King's, and, relaxing in the knowledge that his future education was now assured, he was able to take part in rowing for the school's regatta and gaining the Junior Training Corps' war certificates.

Unexpectedly, during that summer holiday, when school was out, catastrophe came to Hereford, hitherto protected from raids, when two bombs fell on a munitions factory in the Rotherwas part of the city. The factory employed a high number of women; seventeen died and twenty-seven were injured. After that, the Dean of the cathedral, organised a squad of fire watchers which included some of the school's day boys living with their families in Hereford.

Chapter 11
Cambridge

When Joe went up to Cambridge, and specifically to King's College, at the beginning of October 1943, he found that, despite the war, college life was continuing as normal. Many senior members had gone off to the forces or to the civil service, but as the government had decided not to call up men under 20 years of age, about three-quarters of the normal numbers were in residence in 1940. However, these spaces in the various Cambridge colleges were more than filled by government departments, by RAF training units and by over two thousand students from colleges of the University of London who remained in Cambridge until the end of the war. Consequently, Joe had to share a large room overlooking the market in St Mary's Place instead of having a room in college. It took him no time at all to notice how extremely cold the East Anglian winters could be with fuel shortages, certainly colder than Herefordshire. Snow fell thickly that year, and biting winds blew in from the continent and across the Fens, creating icicles on the single-paned windows of heatless rooms, and freezing the fingers and toes of even the hardiest students.

Liberated from the protective care and relatively small scene of Hereford Cathedral School, Joe was both thrilled and nervous to stand alone as an adult ready to determine his future at this world-renowned college, intent on doing his best, out of personal pride, to justify his scholarship and to please his parents. He was, after all, only seventeen years old. In the holidays he had listened attentively to Aunt Leah recalling her days at Warsaw University and her impressions there, which unfortunately were depressing in that she decided to leave owing to rampant antisemitism. It was after that negative experience that she attended a concert in which Mark Lewandowski from England was the guest baritone. She fell in love with his voice, he fell in love with her and eventually they were married, settling in St. John's Wood.

Unlike Leah, Joe did not anticipate antisemitism in Cambridge. There were plenty of Jewish students in all the faculties, Jewish lecturers and an active Cambridge University Jewish Society. On the other hand, he considered himself to be a secular Jew and certainly not Orthodox like many of them; he did not wear a kippah and had, over the years, eaten a great deal of non-kosher food both at school and from Aunt Leah's kitchen. She neither kept a kosher home nor attended synagogue. Mark was similarly non-observant, but as a singer and musician, he was the cantor in a well-known London synagogue and conductor of the choir, as well as composing much of the music. Their children had never attended Jewish schools and were pupils at nominally Christian schools in the countryside, well out of the way of bombing paths, although you could never be sure.

On arrival in Cambridge, it was an adventure to

wander down the narrow streets with their large buses, and breathe in the charming character of it all, before heading down towards the vibrant market where produce of all kinds from a very agricultural county was on display. Joe smiled at the undergraduates… scores and scores of them on bicycles, their academic black capes fluttering in the wind. There were others, of course, on foot, hurrying perhaps to the next lecture or returning to college. Again, King's Parade was full of young university men and women on bicycles or on foot.

He'd seen nothing like it before, and his heart missed a beat with excitement as he realised that he was part of this academic community. He'd dearly like to send word to his parents, but knew that it was impossible.

Ian and Eileen Grundy had set Joe up with the extra clothes he needed, including an academic gown, whilst Leah had knitted pullovers and gloves in whatever free time she had after her government work and that of the house, as well as darning his socks during the holidays. This seemed to be an unending task as it involved those of the entire family, and Leah would spend many an evening listening to news on the wireless as she darned or knitted, hoping to hear something positive about the situation in Poland. Sometimes, when the siren moaned out, it became necessary to seek refuge in the Morrison shelter, situated in the basement for extra protection. After the raid was over, Mark would join his friends on fire duty. It was a nerve-wracking time, and despite being a singer, he resorted to smoking to calm his nerves.

The war situation in Cambridge was quite different

from that of St John's Wood. The colleges survived with very little damage throughout the war, although some two hundred incendiary bombs were dropped in and around Parker's Piece in January 1940. They did, however, destroy Perse School and part of the Catholic church, and a Dornier dropped several bombs on the railway sidings on Mill Road, killing twenty-four people. It was thought there was unspoken agreement that if the Luftwaffe did not bomb Oxford and Cambridge, then the RAF would not bomb Heidelberg and Göttingen.

Lectures occurred mainly in the mornings, and then at one p.m. the undergraduates would return to their colleges. In Joe's case his return was to his room in town, to the college cafeteria and then to King's library, until dinner in Hall in the evening. As a Classics scholar, he enjoyed hearing the Latin grace initially, and the chance to get to know other students. There seemed to be more Science undergraduates than those studying the Arts, and by no means all British.

King's College was located in the centre of town, and Joe learned that it was founded by Henry VI at the age of nineteen in 1441, soon after the foundation of Eton, and built in the style of late Gothic English architecture. It was of interest to new undergraduates that the founding of the college was originally for a rector and twelve poor scholars from Eton, and each year the provost and two fellows would impartially select those worthy of a place. In subsequent years the numbers were maintained at seventy... until they further increased.

One Saturday afternoon early on in the term, Joe and

a group of new friends he'd got to know over dinner in Hall went for a walk around parts of Cambridge, starting off with King's Chapel. It was in a sorry state despite its reputation for beauty. The east window had been removed, followed by all the other windows, early on in the war, and stored in various cellars in Cambridge. In winter the Chapel was extremely cold as the windows were replaced with sheets of grey tar paper which rattled thunderously in the wind. The group also learned that many of the adult choristers had been called up for army service, thus reducing the music possibilities of the choir, until practices and rehearsals ceased, except for Christmas concerts.

They strolled on to the back of King's which looked directly onto the River Cam and into a pastoral area called 'The Backs', consisting of the rear grounds of several colleges including St John's, Trinity, Trinity Hall, Clare and Queen's, each with its own bridge over the river. It made a very pleasant walk on a fine day, and in summer an inviting place for study on the banks in the sunshine or rowing on the Cam, they agreed. Joe had met up with some undergraduates from Eton from a prosperous background, but also those from grammar schools and even a sprinkling of refugees from Europe, like himself. His years at Hereford had really helped him to settle into a very English environment. His roommate, Harry Lewis, hailed from nearby Saffron Walden and was reading Maths. They certainly did not have their academic subjects in common, but Joe found Harry to be easy going and friendly with a mischievous sense of humour and a raucous laugh, so that they got on well enough in a spacious room which was fortuitously fitted out with a large cupboard, two desks, chairs, ample shelf space and an inadequate gas fire. With different lecture times and interests, they tended to see each other only at meal times, especially at dinner in Hall.

After a short time, Harry was interested to know about Joe's background, and became seriously shocked when he learned about life for Jews in Berlin from someone who'd really witnessed it, about Kindertransport and that Joe's parents were in Nazi occupied Poland. Even worse that there was now no communication, or way of finding out if they were safe, that you just had to hope for the best.

Harry's tale was much more straightforward, and as he said, far less exciting. He was eighteen months older than Joe, the only son of a Cambridgeshire arable farmer, and there were three women in his life… his mother, his little sister and his girlfriend. When he was called up, he said, he would definitely join the RAF. He pointed out that RAF Debden was located near his farm, and that in September the previous year it had been transferred to the United States Army Air Force. There were about twenty thousand American airmen in East Anglia at that time and when the weather allowed, they were flying Hurricanes and Spitfires to escort the big bombers over Germany. They are great guys, he said, and have been very generous to the local people on rations, and particularly to the children.

On the 1st November 1943, having been admitted to King's College, Joe matriculated, or formerly enrolled into the university, along with the other Freshmen, all wearing gowns... some bought, some borrowed... where they promised to observe the Statutes and Ordinances of the University and to pay due respect and obedience to the Chancellor and other officers of the University. The first few weeks represented a steep learning curve to them all, although they had each received information prior to their arrival. Joe initially studied for the Classical Tripos. This involved Greek and Latin, Classical Literature, Ancient History, Classical Art, Archaeology and Linguistics. A shortage of professors and lecturers created problems in many faculties, due to so many being called up for army service, but Queen Mary College came up from London with both students and lecturers which helped the staffing problem, but it was a difficult time.

A few days after Matriculation, Harry suggested going to celebrate their newly found academic future at The Eagle on Benet Street, which he said was a hangout for pilots and had a terrific atmosphere. It was a new experience for Joe and as he realised later, not one to be missed. It was a large pub, and apart from the regulars, the place was heaving with RAF pilots and personnel and American Army Air Force pilots and airmen, plus a number of Cambridge undergraduates. Conversation buzzed amid frantic ordering of pints, friendly banter and explosions of laughter. In that pub, it seemed, life really was for living, and both Harry and Joe caught the atmosphere of laughing today, as there might not be a tomorrow. As Joe was tasting his first pint, Harry pointed out the pilots' graffiti and names on the walls and ceiling. He was later told by a GI that some of the names were sadly those who had not returned… either shot down and killed or shot down and serving out the rest of the war in a German prisoner of war camp. It was a memorable evening.

Cambridge was fitted out with air raid shelters just like any other vulnerable town or city in England, and the blackout was observed by all, thanks to the ARP. Numerous members of the RAF were accommodated at King's to attend courses there which greatly interested Harry, who had discovered that it was possible to attend those courses and continue with a degree, or to return to finish the degree after the war. He was keen to do his bit for the war effort as soon as possible at the end of the academic year. In 1944, Hitler sent over V1s or Doodlebugs to terrorise those living in the south-east of England and kill thousands of Londoners. These flying bombs did not manage to reach Cambridgeshire. It seemed that their range did include the South Coast, Hertfordshire, Middlesex, Kent and Essex. They did not reach much further north though, except on Christmas Eve 1944 when Doodlebugs were launched from German Heinkels over the North Sea, reaching across Yorkshire and as far as Manchester, and killed or injured a number of people living there. Fortunately, many V1s landed in the North Sea, or into unpopulated areas.

Joe worked hard at his studies and enjoyed the course. For a bit of light relief in the winter and to keep warm, he would go to the cinema at the weekend with a few friends either on the same course or at college. When he returned to London for the holidays, he found the Morrison shelter much in use. After the Blitz, it came as something of a shock to experience a second blitz. To see the bombs buzzing over, their tails flaming, and then stop to become silent before crashing to the ground with their deadly loads, was truly terrifying. Londoners and those in the South East were then to discover the V2 rockets... more lethal still, and so fast they were impossible to see. You just hoped and prayed to keep safe.

Joe continued to hear nothing from his parents in Lodz and hoped they were safe, although he had heard some dreadful news on the wireless. Aunt Leah was in a constant state of worry about her parents and relatives, but she stoically continued with her job, and as the Nazis and the Axis powers started to lose ground, she looked forward to being reunited with her family after the war.

Excellent news arrived in the summer of 1945. Not only had the war in Europe ended, and finally in Asia too, after the bombing of Hiroshima and Nagasaki, but Joe was awarded a first class pass in the classical part of the Tripos. He was truly delighted that his efforts had resulted in such success, and he imagined how pleased and proud his parents would be. A decision to read Modern Languages... Russian... as the second part of the Tripos, to complete the BA, would require two more years at Kings and not one, since it would mean learning the language from scratch to reach degree standard in that time.

After celebrating at The Eagle again with his now rowdy friends who were demob happy after receiving their results, he decided to help out at Harry's farm, at his invitation, picking potatoes and living there for a couple of weeks. It was hard, back-breaking work, but he valued his friendship with Harry, enjoyed the warm family atmosphere at the farm and pocketed the wages gleefully. Most students were perennially hard-up.

Back in London, the joy and relief of winning the war in Europe continued with effusive festivities, despite the fact that the country was broke, heavily in debt to the United States and to Canada, and with an acute housing crisis owing to the bombing of many towns and cities across the country. Victory over Japan was not as personally felt by the population due to its geographical distance, and was overshadowed by the necessary releasing of atomic weapons, causing so much death and agony to the Japanese people. Leah's job with the government ended at the same time as the war, and Mark's concerts around the country with the Council for the Encouragement of Music and the Arts, also came to an end.

When Joe returned to St John's Wood later in the summer of 1945, Leah was extremely distressed about not hearing from her family in Lodz, and regularly in tears. She and Joe went to Bloomsbury House and to the Red Cross several times to find out any information they could about the fate of their relatives, as news was being transmitted from Europe all the time. On each occasion they found that hundreds of pre-war refugees had gathered there in hope. Indeed, some did receive good news, but the vast majority heard nothing, and turned away sadly until the next time… a harrowing experience for all concerned.

Since Leah was the cousin of Joe's father, Jacub, she

and Joe had dozens of members of their family and extended family in common. She was particularly worried about her parents and two younger sisters, but also about the numerous aunts, uncles and cousins with whom she used to spend happy holidays as a child in the Polish countryside. After her marriage to Mark, she had visited them all just once before the war and had luxuriated in their company, feeling secure and happy surrounded by a family who loved her. Was she never to see them again?

News of the mass murders of Jews in the death camps and concentration camps liberated by the Americans, British and Russians... Belzec, Mauthausen, Majdanek, Belson, Ravensbruck, Dachau, Auschwitz, Treblinka, Chelmno and many others... was revealed to the overwhelming horror of all. Pictures of emaciated bodies of those who had died in filth, hunger and disease filled the newspapers and sickened the readers. Yet there was little evidence to be seen of the gassed and cremated millions. Questions were asked, but no answers given. No-one seemed to know anything. Who had escaped, who had survived? Leah and Joe knew that their relatives had spent the war in the city of Lodz, and that was all. They also knew that Jacub was a Zionist, and had hoped that after the war, he would come to England with Miriam to be united with the family, and then move on with Joe to start a new life in Palestine. It was possible. Many Polish Jews had done it.

As the months and years went by, there was still no information, and Leah suffered a nervous breakdown. Tears overwhelmed her at any time as she assumed that forty-five members of her family had died, and, sleepless, she imagined their suffering, developing an unforgiving hatred of the Germans that did not diminish with time. If she was out shopping and happened to admire an ornament or trinket on a department store counter, she was no longer interested once she had discovered that the item was made in West Germany. Her already shaky faith in God completely disintegrated. How could a loving God allow millions of Jews — His chosen people — to die in misery? She would have nothing to do with synagogues and considered those who did to be wasting their time. Since Mark was director of music at a synagogue, he continued to attend, but he shared Leah's sentiments, and when asked by a rabbi what he believed in, he replied that he believed in music... which did not go down well. Fortunately, the couple had made many friends in London and elsewhere in England who were very supportive of Leah for years. She returned their loyal friendship, but never got over her loss.

When Joe returned to King's in October 1945 to begin the modern languages part of the Tripos, he received good news that he had been awarded the Rannoch Prize for proficiency in Greek and Latin which was worth sixty pounds for that year. Then he took on the challenge of learning Russian from scratch to reach university standard in two years which necessitated assiduous study. The fact that he spoke German, Polish, Yiddish and English fluently, and was well versed in Greek and Latin gave him an advantage. He was well practised in tackling a new language and relished the challenge, even if it had a completely different alphabet.

Although the students of London University had returned to their own alma mater, and the RAF cadets had also left, freeing up the accommodation in college, Joe continued to board at his room in St Mary's Place. It was near enough to the hub of all that went on in King's, and he jelled well with the diverse and interesting group of undergraduates living there. Harry, who had left to join the RAF, had now returned to complete his Maths degree, but was residing in college. He and Joe were glad to see each other, as Harry had survived the war.

Joe was seriously disturbed about the fate of his parents, grandparents and all his other relatives, and could not get them out of his mind. He would think about them particularly at night and remain sleepless for many hours, only to feel jaded and exhausted in the morning. The old survival guilt returned. How dare he be alive when so many of his family had died? There was no contact, either, from his mother's family who had left Lodz to live in Warsaw. If they had not returned from Palestine, they would be alive now, he thought. Neither was there news from the Blombergs. He thought about his friend, Sam Blomberg, when they were at school together in Berlin, and cried into his pillow. He cried for them all.

Having gained a first class pass in Classics, he now found that he could not concentrate. He silently persisted with his study, but without much success. His Russian tutor knew of his background and observed his inertia and sadness. It was fortunate that he, too, was Jewish. His parents had fled from the Russian Empire to England at the end of the nineteenth century, and after a great deal of toil as tailors in the East End of London over many years, they had made good. Dr Markoff knew all about the tough side of life and poverty in his childhood, about the persistence of study towards a goal in view, and he was better qualified than most to counsel Joe. He did recommend that Joe should join the University Jewish Society where he would find sympathetic friends and even those, like him, with missing relatives in Europe so that he could talk about the situation as often as he needed. Talking about it was important, and he did receive a warm welcome from the Jewish Society. The members were kind and helpful, and encouraged him to attend synagogue, but by now his form of Judaism was very lax and secular, neglected as it was by years spent in a Christian boarding school. Joe also still treasured a lurking, hopeful suspicion that his parents might turn up following the post-war chaos in Europe involving tens of thousands of displaced persons.

In 1946, after a year's study, Joe was awarded a Certificate of Proficiency for Competent Knowledge in Russian. He then went on to study for the Modern and Medieval Languages Tripos, specialising in Russian and Slavonic languages and achieved a second class pass in the examinations for Part II of this Tripos in 1947. He graduated with a BA on 17th June 1947, and then with an MA in absentia in 1950. His valuable time at Cambridge had come to an end, and, like most of his fellow students, he was both glad and sorry. He would miss their company; the camaraderie and sharing of ideas, the lectures, the humour, the punting on The Backs, and the visits to The Eagle, the cinema and to Harry's farm, but the time had come for them all to follow the next chapter of their lives, although they would keep in touch. He was thankful and grateful to his mother for sending him on the Kindertransport, for saving his life, to Leah and Mark for unofficially adopting him as their son, and to Mr and Mrs Grundy who had provided for his upkeep and education. He thought about the power of evil in the world; it was most definitely there, but goodness was there too.

Chapter 12
Resolutions

When Joe returned to London in the autumn of 1947, he became aware again of the terrible destruction that the Luftwaffe, and more recently the Doodlebugs and V2s, the pilotless rockets, had perpetrated countrywide. Rationing and shortages continued, a Labour government was in power, and prefabricated houses littered the landscape of a once proud city in order to deal with the chronic housing crisis. On the plus side, many jobs were created to rebuild the country, and the NHS was in its infancy.

Despite some near misses in St John's Wood, the Lewandowskis' house had escaped serious bomb damage and had only sustained broken windows from the blast. Mark's relatives in the East End had not fared so well, but at least nobody had lost their lives. They were being rehoused in distant places like Portishead and Southend.

Whilst staying with Ian and Eileen Grundy, who, after the war, had moved back to Acton, Joe discussed with them what he aspired to in the future. In the long term, his wish was to fulfil the dream of his parents and live in Palestine, which according to the Balfour Document was to become a homeland for the Jews, but that nothing would be done "which may prejudice the civil and religious rights of existing non-Jewish communities in Palestine". And thousands of Jews did emigrate to the British Mandate, but owing to riots between Arabs and Jews, combined with British political/economic interests with the Arabs, Jewish immigration had been stringently reduced. Consequently, outright war between the Jews, led by terrorist groups, the Irgun, the Lehi and the Haganah, against the British and the Arabs was creating enormous bloodshed and loss of life. The most heinous act of terrorism was the bombing of the King David Hotel in Jerusalem in 1946. Perpetrated by the Irgun, which caused the deaths of ninety-one people and injured forty-six more. It was hardly the time for emigration. Ian Grundy advised waiting until events calmed down, but in the meantime, what was Joe to do? He was disenchanted with the idea of doing his National Service with the possibility of being sent to Palestine to fight on the side of the British against his own people, although that was an unlikely scenario.

Having considered his options as a linguist, Joe decided he should attend the School of Oriental and African Studies in Bloomsbury, central London, as a research student. He stayed with Mark and Leah and family in St John's Wood, which was always his home base, before being sent to Sierra Leone to study Mende, a major language not only in that country but also in neighbouring Liberia. Returning to London in the summer of 1948, his sketchy knowledge of what had been happening in Palestine during his year in Africa changed, as he caught up on his reading and discussion with his relatives. After so much terrorism and loss of life, the British had decided to leave Palestine, the Mandate was terminated and on 14th May 1948, with the backing of the United Nations and the United States, David Ben Gurion declared the establishment of the State of Israel, amid great rejoicing. Joe also learned that the War of Independence had broken out immediately. The Palestinian Arabs were joined by those of Jordan, Syria, Lebanon, Egypt and Iraq.

Throughout the country tens of thousands of Arabs fled their homes, becoming refugees in Arab countries, and this fact became a catalyst regarding the escalation of Arab–Israeli conflict in the years to come, though some Palestinian Arabs did not leave and others returned later. Heavy losses were sustained on both sides. Over six thousand Israelis were killed, representing one per cent of the population, and fifteen thousand injured. Many of these soldiers were survivors of the Holocaust, fighting for a homeland. The War of Independence was finally concluded by the signing of armistice agreements between Israel and the surrounding Arab states, the last one being with Syria on 20th July 1949. It was considered something of a miracle for this fledgling land of Israel that peace had been achieved… albeit temporarily.

Leah and Joe continued to search for news of their relatives, hoping that the gradual easing of the situation of displaced persons in Europe would enable them to make contact. Four years had passed since the end of the war, and, still having heard nothing, their survival seemed unlikely. Without information, closure was not possible. Much later, after extensive research, it was sad but realistic to deduce that Leah's parents and other aged relatives in Lodz would have been included in the Nazi round-ups of young children and the elderly in 1942 when they were transported to Chelmno camp and gassed by carbon monoxide in the death vans. What happened to the rest of the family was not so clear.

Emigrating to Israel, or making aliyah, was still inadvisable at this stage. The situation in Israel needed to calm down, and Joe needed to earn some money, having been supported financially by Ian and Eileen Grundy since he was thirteen. During one of his visits to them, he learned that the other Kindertransport boy who had shared their home, Rolf Steinberg, had been able to join his sister and other relatives in the United States, but in spite of gaining a diploma from the Royal College of Music, he was now studying to be a doctor in New York. Like most of the Kindertransport children, he had received no news of his parents, and assumed they were dead, though where or when was unknown.

Joe was glad to receive similar fatherly advice from both Ian Grundy and Mark Lewandowski about preparing to go to Israel in the future. His life in England, since 1939, had been spent in school and university, supported, organised and educated. Now he needed to learn to stand on his own feet, earn some money and develop his independence before spending his future in a foreign country. Joe decided to explore Scotland, and with his Cambridge degree he had no difficulty in gaining a post in teaching Classics at Fettes College in Edinburgh.

Chapter 13
The Mass Aliyah

Between the establishment of the State of Israel in May 1948 and the end of 1951 tens of thousands of Jews emigrated to that country. About seventy thousand were survivors of the Holocaust from displaced persons' camps in Germany, Austria and Italy; others had been detained by the British on Cyprus and many thousands returned from China. During this period entire Jewish communities arrived... thirty-seven thousand from Bulgaria, over thirty thousand from Libya, a hundred and twenty-one thousand five hundred and twelve from Iraq, a hundred and three thousand seven hundred and thirty-two from Poland and nearly a hundred and nineteen thousand from Romania.

Absorbing all these people into the country's life was a massive challenge and required substantial financial support from Diaspora Jewry through the Jewish Agency. The majority were settled in towns and villages, some in homes abandoned by Palestinian Arabs and fifty-three thousand in permanent houses. Owing to a huge demand for accommodation, about a hundred and twelve thousand people remained in immigrant camps and temporary housing, and, as the pressure for housing increased, these camps filled to beyond capacity. To alleviate the overcrowding, a system called the ma'abarah, or transitional camp, was devised in which the newcomers were provided with work... which proved to be more successful.

Joe's appointment at Fettes College had been very successful owing to his comprehensive knowledge of the Classics combined with an innate ability to teach well. He concerned himself seriously with the achievement of his students, most of whom gained creditable results at the end of the academic year, and he interacted well with the staff who were sorry to lose him by the summer of 1951. They knew his story, understood his Zionism and appreciated that his stay with them was temporary. Fettes College, and Edinburgh in general, had welcomed him and he warmed to them both and to an attractive young teacher on the staff, but she was not Jewish and he knew that his future lay in Israel. On that point he remained single-minded.

Preparations for Joe's departure were made during the autumn of 1951, and he felt nervous, sad and excited all at the same time, saying goodbye to Ian and Eileen Grundy who had given him such generous support and guidance for nearly twelve years. Childless, these kind, caring people considered Joe and Rolf to be like adopted sons, wanting the best for them, but sad that the inevitable break had finally arrived. Joe promised to keep in touch as they hugged him goodbye, and he would always remember them waving to him from their colourful and fragrant garden as he headed for the bus to take him back to St John's Wood. It was even more emotional at the Lewandowskis' home. The whole family had grown to love Joe, and would miss him, but the children had become young adults and had their own lives to lead. Mark's mind was always on the next concert, a composition, a gifted pupil or perhaps the choral music for the High Holy Days. Although he enjoyed his family, company and conversation, it would be true to say that music was his raison d'être. Leah, on the other hand, more reserved by nature, had withdrawn into her own sad thoughts, and considered Joe to be the last link to her lost family in Poland... which he was. The whole family made their final goodbyes to him at London Airport, promising to stay closely in touch.

The British had given up Lydda Airport when they left Palestine in April 1948. The Israel Defence Force had captured the airport in July of that year and regular services to and from London were started in 1950. Joe flew in from London to Tel Aviv, which was renamed the David Ben Gurion International Airport in 1973, as it is known today.

The Jewish Agency had set up a central immigrant processing camp known as Shaar Haaliya, near Haifa in the north of Israel. It was isolated and fenced off for health purposes and served as a quarantine area. Whether immigrants arrived by air, land or by sea, they were destined to make their way to Shaar Haaliya. Joe travelled there by truck from the airport, like all the other immigrants, and noted the stark contrast of climate between Haifa and chilly Edinburgh or London, needing to shed his coat and pullover in the afternoon sunshine.

The first hurdle of processing an immigrant was registration at the reception area, involving passport number, age, country of origin, profession, if any, and marital status. When Joe arrived, the area was swarming with people of many nations, ages and abilities, waiting for their turn; children were crying, standing in mud outside inadequate tents, and the elderly looked exhausted and confused, seemingly oblivious to all the noise around them, much of it in the form of complaints. The more vocal of the arrivals objected to the quarantine area owing to the isolation, barbed wire fences and police with dogs which reminded them of the Holocaust, and they refused to cooperate with it. The truth was that the health authorities, dealing with hundreds of people each day, needed to know about individual health problems as well as potential epidemics. Nobody would be sent away, but nobody could leave until they had satisfied the doctors what treatment they needed, if any. Each health problem would be dealt with, and it was seemingly a huge, never-ending task. Yet for many people, Shaar Haaliya was simply a processing station.

Unlike the fate of many others, Joe's processing took only two days, but whilst waiting for his medical examination, he was required to share accommodation with scores of men and boys in a large dormitory with countless narrow beds and no privacy. Women and children shared a similar dormitory. The vile conditions of Nazi concentration camps had become public knowledge since 1945, and so Joe now had an inkling of what life was like being surrounded by so many people… the noise, the dirt, the arguments, the smells, the snoring… except, of course, they were welcomed and not abused, the inconvenience was temporary, there was no shortage of food and the beds were not tiered. Israel was to be their land, and they would never be persecuted again. Joe was glad to be an immigrant, and in talking to those around him he began to understand something of the hell they had endured: how they had clung to life, lost many close relatives and still felt very guilty for having survived. Some looked as if they were only just holding onto the thread of life. He asked them about Lodz in the slim hope of gaining information about Jacub and Miriam, but without success.

Joe passed his medical examination with no difficulty, was pronounced fit and healthy and before leaving the health centre was given an anti-tuberculosis vaccination. Evidently that disease was rife among many of those who had been in the camps, and they could quite easily pass the disease on to others without realising it. Going through customs was easy since he had nothing to declare, and then his future service in the Israel Defence Force was discussed. He would need to immerse himself in a five-month course of Hebrew initially before being called up by the IDF. As he was on his own, unencumbered by family, it was straightforward for him to join a truck bound for Ulpan Etzion in Jerusalem where he could learn Hebrew and benefit from the accommodation there.

As the truck approached Jerusalem, Joe felt tears trickling down his face. So many thoughts and emotions crowded his mind. Here, he was in the holiest city for Jews, a place where his parents had longed to live out their lives, yet evil had prevented them. He still had no idea what had become of them. By the end of the war they would have still been in their forties. He felt the anger rise in his throat. He bit his lip, wiped away his tears and noticed the Dome of the Rock dominating the city in the morning sunshine. Nobody in the truck spoke to him. They all had their own thoughts and emotions and were silent until they reached the language school.

The welcome at Ulpan Etzion was warm and business-like. After registration and the organisation of sleeping accommodation, Joe found himself with twenty others in a classroom. First of all, they were told that ancient Hebrew had been modernised and revived by Eliezer Ben Yehuda as a mother tongue in the late nineteenth century and early twentieth century, and that the Ulpan course was created to help immigrants learn the Hebrew language and to assimilate into the culture. Etzion was the first language school, but soon the Ulpanim would mushroom all over the country, even in the army and the kibbutzim, all based on the Etzion model in Jerusalem so that immigrants could benefit from intensive study of Hebrew for five months.

Having had some teaching experience himself, Joe was very interested in the Ulpan technique of total immersion and the constant involvement of the student in the learning process. Everyone participated in speaking, reading and writing skills, interacting with each other as well as with the teacher. Interestingly they were taught phrases needed to converse, as well as vocabulary and grammar applied with practical use. After class the group diligently practised what they had learned and refused to lapse into their mother tongues which caused a great deal of fun at first when having to resort to sign language in order to communicate. With twenty-eight hours of instruction each week, and after five months, an active vocabulary of two thousand words was the goal. The group bonded, lasting friendships were made, and everyone agreed that Ulpan Etzion had been a very valuable and fun experience.

Towards the end of the course, Joe thought he recognised a woman from another course having lunch in the canteen. Although shy and reserved by nature, he felt the urge to speak to her, remembering that he had seen her before, but where? Then he quickly realised it was from a photo in the living room in St John's Wood. He approached her, introduced himself, and what followed was overwhelming for them both. Hebrew was temporarily forsaken for Yiddish and Polish as they caught up on so much news. Her name was Ruszka, and she was indeed Leah's sister. Before the outbreak of war, she had met and married a Bulgarian national and they had both gone to live in Sofia. During the war she had given birth to a daughter, Ani, but unfortunately later her husband had died, so there was no future for them in Bulgaria. Nevertheless, she was aware that the King of Bulgaria and the Church had refused to hand over the Bulgarian Jews to the Nazis, which certainly did not happen in Poland, France, Hungary, Slovakia and other European countries. Following the declaration of the State of Israel and, thanks to the Jewish Agency, she joined thousands of Bulgarian Jews settling in Israel.

Joe had witnessed his Aunt Leah's bitter tears about the loss of her family on many occasions. Mark had even written a song for her entitled 'Weep No More', willing her to come to terms with the sorrow and find some joy in life again. Joe wrote to her the same day, telling her that he had not only discovered her sister, Ruszka, but also her niece, Ani, too. It was an emotional time of hope at her deliverance, and for Leah's sake, his tears fell again as he was writing the letter giving her Ruszka's address. If only he could come across his parents in a similar way.

As expected, the Ulpan course proved immensely successful for both Joe and Ruszka, enabling them to understand, to make themselves understood and to fit into the Israeli culture. Ruszka was a pianist by profession, but temporarily worked on a kibbutz close to Jerusalem. Ani loved the communal life with the other children at school there and would learn the language quickly in class. After a year she would speak fluently. Joe was delighted to visit them at the kibbutz and noticed that physically it was a hard life, but a worthwhile one. So many people with degrees and doctorates were happy to serve Israel, working in the fields to boost the economy.

Back in England, Leah was roused from her melancholy on receiving Joe's letter, and soon made arrangements to fly to Israel to be reunited with Ruszka and to meet little Ani. Mark had several work commitments, so he was unable to accompany her. The two sisters would talk non-stop and catch up on the news of several years. It turned out to be a wonderful time of joyful reunion to them both, and plans were made for

Ruszka and Ani to visit London in the future when they could. In the meantime, they would correspond regularly. Joe noticed a new lightness in his Aunt Leah's demeanour, unseen for many years, although her sister was unable to tell her what had happened to the rest of the family in Lodz. She simply did not have the facts, but she could guess.

After the course, and empowered by her knowledge of Hebrew, Ruszka gained a job as *repetiteur* at the budding Tel Aviv Opera Company. She and Ani left the kibbutz for a flat in Tel Aviv, and Ani went to school locally. They were both delighted with the vitality of the city, and its location next to the sea.

Chapter 14
The IDF and the Future.

It was not long after the Ulpan course that Joe was contacted by the Israel Defence Force for army service, but before that he made contact with the Hebrew University of Jerusalem on Mount Scopus. The professors were impressed with his qualifications in both the Classics and in Russian and Slavic languages, but practically speaking they were more interested in his joining the English Faculty, and advised him to revisit the university after his army service with that in mind. That would be in three years' time!

The IDF was founded in May 1948, immediately after the declaration of the State of Israel, and since then had become a compulsory military service which was particularly necessary in the early years when the country was fighting for its existence and needed every soldier it could recruit; men for three years, women for two. When Joe enlisted in 1952 the situation was very much the same. Soldiers were needed. Induction Centres were situated all around the country and Joe enrolled in the Jerusalem area. Then, like all drafted soldiers, he was sent to Bakum, the Central Processing Centre for all new recruits and situated in Tel Hashomer, a neighbourhood of Ramat Gan, about seven kilometres to the south-east of Tel Aviv, where he was supplied with a uniform and basic gear and questioned about his education and qualifications, undergoing cognitive and personality tests. It was crucial to both the IDF and the individual that talents were used effectively. Joe was assigned to one of the Intelligence Departments, but before that he had to undergo basic training like all Israeli Army recruits.

The days were designed to toughen up the new recruits and to teach them the art of soldiering. Some had only just left their parents, whereas many others seemed born for the army and adopted a more independent and assertive attitude. The officers insisted on speaking Hebrew during the day, but out of hours they lapsed into English, French or Russian, depending on their mother tongue. For Joe it was an opportunity to practise all three, as well as Hebrew.

In those early years of so much immigration, many recruits were unexpectedly reunited with those they had thought had perished in the camps. Some looked down the lists for names they recognised in the hope of finding someone they knew, and when they did, tears and jubilation reigned. This happened particularly among Polish and Russian Jews who, for survival during the war, had perhaps changed their identities, sought the help of priests and nuns, or gone into hiding and not been discovered; they may even have joined the partisans and lived in forests until the danger was over.

Joe was cheered to witness these heartfelt reunions, but since he was German by birth and had spent all the war years in England, he did not expect any such reunion would apply to him, and felt rather solitary. He was therefore surprised one evening after training when a slight, young soldier asked him if his name was Josef Mendelson and did he come from London? He introduced himself as Dov Friedman who had spent the war in Lodz and knew Joe's family; in fact, after the death of his own parents, he had actually lived with them and had particularly appreciated the kindness of Grandmother who later had sadly died. He also mentioned that he knew about the Kindertransport, and how much Jacub and Miriam were looking forward to being with Joe in London. He provided Joe with an account of the hellish conditions of life in the Lodz ghetto particularly in the summer of 1944. Hans Biebow, the German chief of the ghetto was keen to keep the Jews operational in the factories because he had grown rich on their efforts, but since all the other ghettos had already been liquidated, Heinrich Himmler pulled rank and insisted that the remaining thousands should be sent to Auschwitz as soon as possible, particularly as the Chelmno gas vans were considered slow and inefficient. And so, the Einsatzgruppen were rounding up thousands of Jews every day and transporting them off to Auschwitz. He explained how he had evaded the Nazi search for him, but actually witnessed seeing Ezra, Sara, Jacub and Miriam being taken to the Radogoszcz station. Destination: Auschwitz.

Dov explained, too, how he had stayed in hiding in the ghetto, moving from one clandestine hole to another, until the Nazis had rounded up the last few thousands, and then left between seven hundred and fifty and eight hundred people behind, whose job it was to clear and clean up the ghetto. After the work was completed, they too would be killed, since the Nazis had forced them to dig shallow, rectangular pits into which their corpses would be dumped. But in the meantime, meagre food rations would be supplied, and Dov was able to become part of that group. Fortunately, the fat member of the Einsatzgruppen, who had pursued him on that fateful day (when the Mendelsons had been forced from their apartment) and who would have recognised him, had been moved on elsewhere when the rounding up was over, for which Dov was very grateful. He was able to use his wits to help other Jews, and was glad of their company.

Joe listened in silence as Dov told him about the freezing months of December and January, how his private stock of food had dwindled to nothing, how the 'cleaners' were terrified that the Nazis would change their minds and shoot them all or send them off to Auschwitz. They finally learned that all the cleaning of the apartments was to accommodate German personnel returning from the East, so they prolonged their efforts as they heard the thunder of Russian artillery every day. At first, the Soviets had made tremendous progress marching through eastern Poland, and they could hear the artillery coming nearer and nearer, but then it stopped near Warsaw waiting for the Polish uprising which took several weeks. Only then, he said, did they travel west to reach Lodz on the 19th January 1945. The Nazis had clearly underestimated the Soviets, and certainly about eight hundred lives in Lodz had been saved by their arrival. Then many more lives were saved when

Auschwitz was liberated at the end of the same month. Too late for Miriam, Jakub and his parents Ezra and Sara.

Joe asked about the Warsaw ghetto, knowing that a number of his mother's relatives had set up home there before the war. Dov replied that they would have ended up in Treblinka and not Auschwitz, since it was nearer to Warsaw. Joe sat, his head in his hands, sickened by the suffering of his family, and by the wider family... the Jewish family. Then he thought about the catastrophic decision his mother's relatives had made returning to Poland from Palestine in the 1930s. If they had stayed, they would be alive now. The whole lot had been wiped out; only he and Ruszka remained.

Dov was small, tough and gutsy, a quick-witted Polish Jew, totally without relatives, like many others, but ready to serve his new country with all his might, on the front line of the IDF if necessary; he was truly inspirational to Joe who observed all the diverse talents around him and realised that Israel needed every single one. Eventually he would be a teacher and academic for Israel, but Dov would be a professional soldier, he was sure. He was also sure that many of those recruits around him had heartbreaking stories they could tell, yet here they were, gaining strength from each other, dancing in the induction yard and singing "Am Yisrael Chai" — "Israel lives!" The resilience of the human spirit was truly breathtaking.

Joe served his three years in Military Intelligence, and the main work was to supply the Israeli government and the IDF with Intelligence warnings and alerts on a daily basis. This involved processing and evaluating

Intelligence information, and transmitting it to the appropriate places in order to track terrorist activities. It was important work, and Joe applied himself to it with considerable concentration and secrecy. He learned a great deal, worked hard and made many friends, keeping in contact with Ruszka, Ani and Dov in Israel, but also with the Lewandowskis, together with Ian and Eileen Grundy in England. Then every so often he would hear from Rolf Steinberg who had qualified as a doctor in New York, or from friends in Cambridge and Hereford.

The time passed rather quickly, more quickly than he had imagined, mainly because of the importance of the work and the camaraderie of those around him, both male and female. Most of the young soldiers were secular or Orthodox, but no Ultra-Orthodox Jews were obviously serving in the army. Following the Holocaust, the vast majority of the Hasidim had been wiped out by the Nazi regime, so the Israeli government excused them from joining the IDF. Instead they studied the Torah and the Talmud and brought a marked spirituality to the country.

Reserve army service was mandatory in the 1950s, understandable when the country was surrounded by Arab nations intent on Israel's destruction. In those early days, reserve service amounted to about one month a year, sometimes more, and a large part of the Israeli population served in the IDF. They were used to receiving special call-up letters sent to reservists' postal addresses, telling them when and where to report.

It was towards the end of Joe's three years with the IDF, working as head of his Intelligence Section, that

Margalit Meyer returned for reserve service and found herself working with him. In fact, for that month, Joe was her boss. By now she could speak Hebrew fluently, as well as German, English and Russian, and had already spent two years working in Intelligence since she had arrived in Israel with her mother and sister in 1949. She was quite tall, slim, attractive and quick-witted, with a winning smile and a relaxed way of speaking. And, of course, unmarried. Joe was attracted to her both mentally and physically; they were on the same wave length, but in all these years, he had only mixed with women in a group, at work and in the army. He felt rather shy and wished he was not, disciplining himself to keep his mind on the work since it was so important to the national interest, and nothing should compromise it. So, he waited until her last day of reserve army service, mustered up courage as she was about to leave, and she accepted his invitation to dinner.

It was as if they had both been searching for that special person for several years without realising or admitting it, and suddenly their unspoken dream became reality. They had found each other at last, and there was so much to talk about, so much in common as German Jews who had fled in different directions before the war, he to England and she to China, and here they were, falling in love and in Israel, the country they had both yearned to be part of for many years.

The more time they spent with each other, the harder it was to part. Margalit returned to her job as a paediatric nurse working for WIZO (the Women's International Zionist Organisation) in the department of premature

141

babies… a job she loved… but sometimes she would weep at night with loneliness, longing for Joe's arms to be around her, and she crossed off the days when she would see him next. Many people had treated Joe with generous help and encouragement over the years, but now what he wanted most was the love of his own close family, missing from his life since 1939 and wiped out in the war. Whenever he saw Margalit, the feelings of isolation, of bereavement and emotional self-discipline were replaced by closeness and love. He laughed more and opened up his heart as he would never have thought possible, and, once again, he pondered the love and courageous decision of his mother who had saved him for a life of fulfilment and happiness. He was by now nearly thirty years old, and completely overwhelmed by this unexpected feeling of inner joy. As twin souls, both he and Margalit wanted to marry as soon as possible; there was no reason to wait, and their need for each other was great.

As they were short of cash, a modest wedding was arranged and they both invited those in Israel who were important to them. On Joe's side it was Ruszka, Ani and Dov; from Margalit's side, her mother, sister and brother-in-law, plus a few mutual friends from the IDF. Warm greetings and wedding gifts were sent from Ian and Eileen Grundy and from the Lewandowskis who, in years to come, would visit them in Jerusalem and would celebrate a wonderful reunion together.

Before the marriage, Joe had managed to rent a bijou flat situated near the Hebrew University of Jerusalem where he was employed in the English Faculty, and

Margalit continued to work for WIZO until she became heavily pregnant with her first child. They were truly happy together and founded the family so important to them both, raising three sons. In 1958, the university sent Joe to Oxford for two years to study for his doctorate, and of course the family went too. Many years later, he became a highly-respected professor of English, always a private man of unpretentious wisdom and humanity, and devoted to his family, colleagues and students. He registered his parents' and grandparents' murders in Auschwitz at Yad Vashem. Hitler and his evil cohorts had done their worst, but the children of Israel would still number the stars. L'Chaim! To Life!